Pay Attention

Sex, Death, and Science

Also by John Horgan

The End of Science

The Undiscovered Mind

Rational Mysticism

The End of War

Mind-Body Problems

Pay Attention

Sex, Death, and Science

John
Horgan

Terra Nova Press
NEWARK   CALLICOON   MATSALU

2020

© 2020 by John Horgan
ISBN 978-1-949597-09-7
Library of Congress Control Number: 2020941945

Published by:

Terra Nova Press
NEWARK   CALLICOON   MATSALU

Publisher: David Rothenberg
Editor-in-Chief: Evan Eisenberg
Designer: Martin Pedanik
Illustrator and Cover Artist: Nikita Petrov
Proofreader: Tyran Grillo
Set in Giovanni and Space Mono

Printed by Tallinn Book Printers, Tallinn, Estonia

1 2 3 4 5 6 7 8 9 10
www.terranovapress.com

Distributed by the MIT Press, Cambridge, Massachusetts
and London, England

For "Emily," my Dream Girl

Author's Note

About the Author

Further Reading

Author's Note

Like my other books, this is a work of journalism. It describes a day, *circa* 2013, in which I wake up in Cold Spring, New York, commute to a college in Hoboken, New Jersey, and take a ferry to New York City to meet my girlfriend, whom, because she values her privacy, I'll call Emily. I've had many days like this since 2009, when my marriage broke up and I moved into an apartment in Cold Spring.

The book is based on notes I took while commuting, teaching and so on, and on recordings of conversations between me and others. I spliced events from many days into an account of one day, and I changed some details for readability and some names (including mine) for privacy and deniability. So technically, the book is fiction, but it is more true-to-life than anything else I've published.

An early draft was more aggressively stream-of-consciousness-y. One friend described it as unprocessed mental sludge. I set it aside until the summer of 2019, when my pal David Rothenberg told me he was launching a book imprint and looking for material. After I cut the book in half and labored to make it more readable, David and his editor-in-chief, Evan Eisenberg, agreed to publish it. My thanks to them and to "Emily," who thought—and hoped—this book would never see the light of day.

John Horgan, Summer 2020

Chapter 1

Waking Up in Spring Brook Apartments

Who farted? Wait, I did. Did it wake her? No, phew, Emily isn't here. I'm here, alone, in Cold Spring, she is far away, in New York City. I can fart at will, freely, like… now. No, insufficient gas. Farted without intention when sleeping, can't fart now with intention. Free Will so paradoxical!

Did I dream I farted? No, smell confirms it. I stink therefore I am. Good line, should use it in a column, farting as a case study of Free Will. Remember that idea, remember, write it down. If I don't write it down, I don't remember. If I don't remember, it doesn't matter. We invented God to remember everything, but maybe God forgets too. In the long run, everything gets forgotten, nothing matters.

Get my notebook? Write down fart idea? 4:40. No, need more sleep. Lie still, face up, eyes closed, mind empty, think nothing, know nothing, say my magic mantra: Duh… Duh… Duh… Duh…

Morning boner. More likely sleeping alone or with her? That's a potentially answerable question, hence scientific. Strap cuff sensor on penis, with wifi link to laptop, gives you erection timeline. Company that sells Viagra should invent an app for that and give it a punny name. App shows correlation of tumescence to things you do and things that happen to you as you go through your day. Infinite boner variables!

Erection Detection. Yeah, good name for app, remember that. Erection Detection will show boners require more stimulation, imagination, willpower as men age. Don't need much willpower with her, though. Waking in her bed I smell her, feel her, warm, in t-shirt and panties, or just t-shirt, or nothing at all, if she's having hot flashes. Naked woman beside me of her own Free Will.

How long will I get morning boners? Until my last gasp in a nursing home, probably. Nurse discovers my decrepit old carcass in bed, withered and flabby except for penis in rigor mortis. Embarrassing. Who cares, I'll be dead. Upside of death, no more shame.

Oh no: my To Do program starts booting up, against my will, listing things to do, or just to worry about. Reminding me of something, something bad. Ugh, The Fight. She was so unfair! No, can't think about it now, need more sleep. Duh… Duh… Duh…

Dreams last night, remember, remember. Can't remember. Like looking down at a dark pond, seeing outlines, shadows moving under the surface. Can't tell if what's down there is nice or nasty, iridescent rainbow trout or fanged, goggle-eyed lantern fish. Maybe I dreamed about her, and her dream body gave my real body a boner.

Someday scientists might reconstruct dreams from neural signals. Like that old sci-fi flick: a brain-scanner records neural patterns underpinning your subjective experiences of dreams, sex, a heart attack, death. Then the brain stimulator recreates the pattern in someone else, so he feels what you felt. Or she. That would solve the solipsism problem. Escape the prison of yourself, discover what it's like to be someone else. Like a murderer, or your girlfriend. We want to know, don't want to know.

What was that old sci-fi movie? *Brainstorm*. Natalie Wood died mysteriously when they were making it. Pentagon hopes science fiction will soon become reality. True mind reading, mind control, tyranny way beyond Big Brother. And the end of romance. If I know what she's thinking, there's no mystery. No mystery, no love.

Crick said dreams are just side effects of brains discarding unneeded memories, like night-time janitors fanning through skyscrapers, vacuuming carpets, emptying waste baskets, cleaning offices for day workers. Memories are activated during disposal, and the brain makes stories out of them. That's why my dreams are so dumb. Made of garbage.

Freud's wacky steampunk theory much cooler than Crick's. Dreams encrypted messages from enraged, terrified, horny subconscious, messages that the brilliant analyst decodes. Freud's stories so artful, persuasive, turned us into Freudians. Father, I want to kill you. Mother, I want to... *yeahhhhhrrrggg!* Imagination trumps truth, imagination *becomes* truth. Life imitates pseudo-science.

Wish I could become lucid when I'm dreaming, like those weirdos I met in Palo Alto. Oneironauts, swapping tips on how to get lucid, take control of dreams, become a superhero, crush monsters, have sex with celebrities. Controlling your dreams like being a movie director with an infinite special effects budget. Reality becomes whatever you want it to be, imagine it to be. You're the God of your dream world.

Oneironauts wore t-shirts asking, Is This a Dream? Ask all day long and you're more likely to ask when you're dreaming and become lucid. Buddhists say enlightenment is waking from reality, realizing it's just a dream. That explains why gurus act like sociopaths. Like Trungpa, getting shitfaced, fucking worshipers, taking their money, haranguing them about *their* egos. If life is just a dream, why bother being nice? Do what you like, nothing matters.

What would it feel like to be a sociopathic guru? No shame, fear, empathy, you don't give a shit about anyone, anything. Can't get more free than that. Kevin says transcranial magnetic stimulation can induce short-term sociopathy. Doubtful, probably placebo effect, but worth trying, could get a column out of it.

Did Mom hear Jim Morrison's primal Oedipal scream as she walked past her teenage son's room? Mom triggered my primal sexual trauma—when I played with Nancy and Molly, neighbors on Princes Pine Road, lying on soft needles in the grove near my house, naked, peering, prying, poking. Children having fun. Mom appears, looms over us, orders us to put clothes on, sends Nancy and Molly home. Grabs my hand, marches me back to the house. My face hot, burning, I did something bad, sinful. What was I, five, six? Sex still feels sinful, like I'm getting away with something.

Duh… Duh…

Pressure sensor in bladder signaling brain: time to take a leak.
Not urgent, I can choose not to go, for now. I went, what, two,
three hours ago? Another old-guy thing, pissing in the night.
Stepping stone to incontinence, impotence, dementia, death. I
can slow down deterioration with reading glasses, hearing aids,
artificial hips, push-ups and sit-ups, willpower. But I can't stop it.

Dad's still lifting barbells at 89, cracking dirty jokes,
embarrassing Rhonda, even after his stroke. Talking to Rhonda
one morning and his words came out all scrambled. He got
mad, thought she was pretending not to understand him. He
got his speech back but still struggles, grimaces as he tries to
dislodge words from his stubborn old brain.

Dad and Rhonda adore Emily, she adores them, tells me I
should appreciate them more. Emily loved her father, but he
wasn't around much, a hard-living guy whose heart quit in
middle age. Emily's mother was so cruel to her that she left
home at 16. Her mother is still alive, in New York, but Emily
hasn't talked to her in years.

After Dad's stroke I said to Emily, What would I be without
words? All glum, serious. She smirked, wiggled her hips, slid
her fingertips over my belly: You'd still be my Monkey Man.
She loves coining labels, nicknames, for me and other animals.
Sees a chihuahua pitter-pattering down the street and cries,
The Cuteness! She called me Science Man right after we met,
then decided I wasn't that sciencey, came up with other names.
Monkey Man, Mr. Magoo. She calls our breakup The Dumping,
reminds me of it every time she gets mad at me. Like last week,
during The Fight.

I was trying to do something nice! Bought ravioli for us at
Whole Foods, spinach and cheese, no meat for my vegetarian

girlfriend. In the checkout aisle, I spotted a treat I knew she loved. Gave it to her that night, proudly, and her face lit up, then darkened. Are you kidding me? Raisins dipped in white chocolate? First of all, how many times have I told you, I hate raisins! And white chocolate! And do you actually not remember the last time you gave me these? Right before you dumped me! I said, Come on, I was just trying to do something nice! I knew raisins dipped in white chocolate had emotional significance for you, I just forgot the significance was bad. Give me a break, the thought is what counts. Yes, Eamon, you're right, the thought is what counts, and once again you were thoughtless. And then the old refrain about The Coldness, I never really listen to her, I'm self-absorbed, stuck in my own little world, blah blah blah.

Tricia said that too. I'm thoughtless, care more about ideas and words than her and the kids. If the ex-wife and girlfriend both say it, does that make it objective? True?

No, they're both wrong.

Whistle from afar. Train filled with sleepy workers winding south along the Hudson. I'll be on the train soon, trekking to New York, then Hoboken, then back to New York, Emily's place. Like the Odyssey, except shorter, less perilous. Would I want more adventures, like Odysseus? Nah, life's hard enough without war, Cyclops, Scylla and Charybdis, bad men trying to kill me and steal my girlfriend. I'm a lover, not a warrior.

Not much of a lover either, Emily says. I confuse love and sex, one of my many flaws. What about hers! She's judgmental, blunt, bossy, makes me feel guilty for eating a lousy hamburger. Believes in pseudo-scientific crap. Astrology, tarot cards, homeopathy.

I apologized for the raisins and white chocolate, said I should have remembered she didn't like them, I fucked up, sorry. She seems to think I'm sincere, licks her upper lip and kisses me. I kiss her back, press against her, she shakes her head, pushes me away, annoyed. No make-up sex that night, or next morning.

My happiness depends too much on her whims, her moods. That's probably why Buddha dumped his wife and became a monk. When he went home after discovering the solution to all suffering, did Buddha's wife give him a hard time about The Dumping? Not to compare myself to Buddha. But still.

Birds chirping, singing. Is bird song an evolutionary adaptation? Does singing help birds make more birds? Or do birds sing for the sake of singing, like David says? They sing to express joy that another day has come. That's what we're here for too. To feel joy, express joy, not just make copies of ourselves. Why then do we feel joy so rarely? That's a serious design flaw. I'm not joyful. Cautiously hopeful, at best. How much hope can we have when we're all doomed? I have flashes of happy forgetfulness with Emily. Minutes go by when I forget myself, my fears, the end of everything.

Should I ask her The Question tonight? What if she says yes?

5:17, might as well turn off the alarm. Where are my glasses? I need glasses to find glasses, light to find light. Loopy paradoxes all around us. You need words to define words, people to make people. Who made the first person? Spoke the first word? Like that drawing of two hands drawing each other. And who drew the artist? Hofstadter's right, it's strange loops all the way down.

What's on today's To Do list? Freshman Humanities this morning. What's the reading for this week? Freud. No, Freud

7

is next week, today is James, "Stream of Thought." Then lunch with Jim. And I have to decide what to blog about this week. Could defend Nagel, agree with him about science turning into ultra-reductionist-materialist-determinist-atheist cult, a cult that denigrates the mysteries of life and consciousness. Yeah, bash Scientific Fundamentalism, science becoming arrogant, betraying the scientific spirit. Science must be humble, self-critical, self-doubting, or it's not science.

Nagel will think, With friends like this guy Eamon Toole...

As my marriage collapsed, my To Do program went haywire, like a sadistic secretary sitting behind a desk in my head, perkily reminding me as soon as I woke, Hello Mr. Toole, don't forget to write boring drivel for your blog today, and be a lousy husband, father, teacher. Over and over during the day, Sadistic Secretary tormented me. Oh, and Mr. Toole, remember you're getting old, your body is falling apart, you're going to be dead before long, might as well ignore your wife and kids and drink yourself into a stupor again tonight, you pathetic piece of shit.

Then what I dreaded most happened. Tricia and I split up. Jim said, I didn't think you were a divorce kind of guy. I said, I didn't think so either. Tricia, Neal, Claire stayed in the house, I rented this furnished apartment in town, near the kids' high school. But things got better. I quit drinking, joined Match.com, met Emily, who can't drink, a genetic thing, alcohol makes her sick. I calmed down, became happy, less unhappy, capable of forgetting myself. Sadistic Secretary retired and moved to Florida. My To Do program became functional again, more under my control.

I started adding Pay Attention to the bottom of my To Do list. Joke but not a joke. That's all enlightenment is, that Zen Master said, Attention. What was his name? Icky You. How do you Pay Attention? Sit still, Buddhists say, stop thinking. I add my own twist, saying Duh over and over, on the out-breath. But meditation doesn't work for me. It's only good for getting to sleep, and not even then. Do other people feel phony when they meditate?

Psychedelics can open up your eyes, but they're risky. My Big Drug Trip back in '81 blew the doors of perception off their hinges. Out of my mind for 24 hours, flashbacks for months, scary psychotic shit. Life just a dream, I thought, and if I wake up everything will vanish. That Harvard guy said the drug sounded like BZ, chemical incapacitant the Pentagon tested on soldiers back in the '60s.

9/11 made me Pay Attention. Tricia and I heard radio reports, ran up the hill behind our house, looked south toward the Manhattan skyline, beyond the curving shining Hudson, and we saw only smoke where the Twin Towers had been. Walking back home, every tree, weed, flower, patch of moss, lichen-crusted stone seemed etched, spot-lit, quivering with significance.

Cancer made Denny Pay Attention. My old high school buddy, a skinny kid who grew up into a big tough man, an engineer, built subway stations in D.C., once punched a crooked contractor. Ladies loved Denny, he loved them, that was hard on his wife, but he was a good provider for her and their kids. Got terminal cancer in his forties. Denny bitter at first, but as his body decayed, he felt a weird affection for life, more than affection, love really, everything looked beautiful, amazing, like when he first took acid in high school. He was so grateful for his wife, kids, life. Denny told me all this lying on his bed, a strong, handsome man who was hairless now, hollow-eyed, skin yellow, blotchy, sagging. Weeks away from death, about to lose everything. Grateful.

Writing is a better way to Pay Attention than a chemical warfare agent, terrorist attack, cancer. Why not start today? Right now? Pay Attention. Observe things, including my own thoughts, think about them, write them down. Who, what is the thinker if you're thinking about your thinking? What is the subject if the subject is the object? Like you're on an Escher staircase, going round and round and up and down, ending up where you started, and that's okay. Don't get bogged down in paradoxes, Zen koan crap. Just observe, record, do your best.

5:37. Shit!

Pad on achy feet into kitchen, fill kettle, turn on stove. Don't turn on the ceiling light in case neighbors across the courtyard look this way. I'm thinking of their well-being, don't want to expose them to the sight of a hairy aging man in boxers. Tricia and Emily are wrong about me. I am deep down a thoughtful, caring, good man. I'm only mean to scientists who deserve it.

Spoon teaspoons of freeze-dried coffee into mug. The Taster's Choice container is curvy, like the torso of a voluptuous woman. Mae West, Scarlett Johansson. The manufacturer of Taster's Choice is manipulating me with subliminal sexual suggestion. Column idea: Taster's Choice and the Problem of Free Will. Or: Did I Really Choose to Buy Taster's Choice?

Still dark outside. Cop car, lights on, cruises slowly down Fair Street in search of wrongdoing. No crime here, officer! Just a humble science writer starting his day. Do Cold Spring cops yearn for crime? Cold Spring is too nice, bland, boring. Like Utopia, Heaven. That's why God dreamed up such a fucked-up world, to make things interesting. No one wants to see a movie about Utopia or Heaven, unless a monster is on the loose.

Kettle hisses and rattles. Turn the burner off, flick the kettle open, pour steaming water into the mug. Gurgle pitch rises as black liquid surges in mug, familiar morning music. Feel anticipatory caffeine buzz while carrying mug and laptop into living room. Does buzz now mean lethargy later? I have irrational faith in conservation laws, probably related to Catholic upbringing. Conservation of Mental Energy, Conservation of Misery. Feel good now, pay for it later, with exhaustion, guilt.

Check email? Twitter and Facebook? No, resist compulsion, addiction to all that internet crap. Sit on couch, write profound thoughts in notebook. Pay Attention. Yeah! Assert autonomy, freedom from machines, capitalist digital mind-controllers!

Just a quick look at email. Croatian guy wants me to read his e-book: The Quantum Unified Field Theory and the Holy Spirit. Sorry Croatian Crank, you get fast delete. Cranks see me as a kindred spirit because I bash mainstream science, but I am not a Crank! I am a rational, hard-nosed critic of science who holds it to very high standards.

Could all the Cranks who see me as a kindred spirit be wrong?

Message from Jim, sent late last night: *Still on for lunch Tuesday?* I reply: *Sure. Stop by my office.* These tiny symbol strings, underpinned by trickles of electrons, alter the trajectories of me and my buddy Jim. We are physical creatures who transcend the physical stuff of which we are made and hence are not ruled by it. We have choices. Like I said in my last Free Will column.

No message from her. Is she still mad about the raisins and white chocolate? No, she's probably not up yet, asleep in her bed. Wish I was with her.

Check Facebook, Twitter for chatter on Free Will column? Mostly negative when I checked last night, maybe nicer comments this morning.

Stop! Enough frittering time away on digital diversions! Pay Attention to Reality! Set laptop aside, pick up notebook and pen, write: Pay Attention. Obey myself, contemplate surroundings. Couch covered with baggy tan corduroy slipcover. Emily made me buy this slipcover to conceal the underlying shit-brown fabric speckled with piss-yellow flowers and patched with duct tape. This couch is like a fat old dead guy in a body bag, and I'm a monk practicing corpse meditation.

On the wall to my right hangs a dancing tin skeleton couple. Gal with pigtails in a skirt, guy in shorts and sombrero, tongue-kissing, kicking up their bony heels. I bought this *memento mori* when I was with Emily in Santa Fe. Day of the Dead version of her and me. We defy you Death! We laugh in your face! Buddha sits on the bookcase, porcelain skin, crinkly eyes, pinkish bellybutton, red lips laughing merrily. I'm Enlightened, you're not, Buddha says. Nyah nyah!

Why do I have such mixed feelings about Buddha, and Buddhists? I find them self-absorbed, self-righteous, sanctimonious, but feel kinship with them. Surely not because I am self-absorbed, self-righteous, sanctimonious.

Buddha reminds me of Minsky. Chubby, bald head, mischievous smile, plus Buddhist ideas about the mind. We don't have a single unified self, we have lots of selves chasing different goals. If one self takes over, you go crazy, become a religious or political nut. Minsky feared having his brain hijacked by a monomaniacal self, but he was curious too. Wished he could make backup copies of himself so he could have first-hand experience of faith in Jesus,

Marx, Freud, L. Ron Hubbard. Wait, Minsky liked Freud. Called him the greatest mind theorist ever. Except for Minsky.

Does happiness mean all your mini-selves live in harmony? Like in a democracy? A true democracy, not this American pseudo-democracy. My mind feels more like a benign dictatorship ruled by a central self, a reasonable, amiable, firm but tolerant guy. A suburban dad who gets along with everyone. I'm not that guy, I feel awkward chitchatting with other dads at lacrosse games, school concerts. But I can play the part. There is no real self, only what we pretend to be. Some parts easier to play than others.

Brain cells fully caffeinated now, doing jumping jacks, squat thrusts. I need caffeine to keep up with her in the morning. She wakes up going full speed, words and ideas tumbling out. As a child she spoke so fast her parents kept telling her to slow down. She learned to speak more slowly in social situations, but she doesn't hold back with me. When she wakes up, she's in her wild mode, she says. That's her true self.

I usually wake up before her, make coffee, check email, maybe work on a column, then creep back into her bedroom, tiptoeing so the wooden floor doesn't creak. In the dim light I can't tell if she's awake. I feel a mini-frisson, I'm in a horror flick, and I'm the monster. The sensation feels hard-wired, maybe a vestige of ancestral hunter-gatherer programs for pursuing prey. That's what Evo Psychos would say. Darwinians, like Freudians, good at making shit up.

Last week I saw her dark eyes open, watching me come toward her in the dark. As I slipped under the sheets she asked what I'd been up to. Writing about Free Will, I said. Boring, she said, you should write about things people care about. Like what? I asked. Like health, she said, or sex. Good idea, I said, burrowing under the sheets, nuzzling her soft warm belly. What are you doing, Monkey Man? she asked. Research, I replied. I waited for her to say Stop! and push me away, but she arched her pelvis and said, Mmmm.

Go back into the bathroom, slip off boxers, sit on the toilet. No time for that, I'm seeing her tonight, should save myself, just in case. Conservation of Sexual Energy. Shave and brush teeth in the shower to save time. I'm always looking for multi-tasking efficiencies, Timesavers. Go over To Do list while sitting on the toilet. Do sit-ups while listening to CNN multiracial beauty report on mass shooting. Talk to Emily while checking email.

Something silly about Timesavers. I'm minute-wise, hour-foolish. I waste days, months, watching TV. Especially after moving into this apartment. My sad little bachelor apartment, Emily calls it. Tricia didn't like watching TV, so when I moved into my own place I exulted in my freedom. Joined Netflix, plowed through *Battlestar Galactica* and *Lost*, sprawled on the couch, alone. And what does it mean to save time? You have more time for things that really matter, that make life worth living. And what things are those? Thinking deep thoughts, writing them down, being with those you love, blah blah blah. What else matters? Hockey, when my team wins. Teaching, on good days. Buddhists say Pay Attention to every moment, even when you're just killing time, or doing stuff you'd rather not do. Chop wood, carry water. Take crap, grade paper.

Head back into bedroom, put on clean boxers, socks, shirt, jeans. A month or two after I met Emily, she told me men don't tuck in shirts anymore. After brief resistance, I started leaving my shirt tails out. Then she mocked my old jeans, said they were too short, urged me to get longer jeans and roll up the cuffs. I resisted again, said rolled-up cuffs are dorky. For weeks she pointed out Manhattan hipsters in jeans with rolled up cuffs. I gave in. I want to believe I'm a man of principle, firm, autonomous, choosing my own course, like a Hemingway hero. Ha. I shall wear the bottom of my trousers rolled, if it makes my bossy girlfriend happy.

Check email, Twitter, Facebook one more time? No, too late, quit being so compulsive, you fucking digital junkie. Load laptop and notebook into backpack. Scan kitchen. Forgetting anything? Black oblong object on the counter. Yeah, bring the digital recorder! Record stuff that happens today, like my freshman class, lunch with Jim, maybe even chitchat with Emily. Raw data for Pay Attention Project. Maybe I can get blog posts out of this. Or a book!

Can a digital recorder think? Is it like anything to be a Sony digital audio recorder? Chalmers would say yes. Anything that processes information, even a thermostat, is conscious. Come on! *Reductio ad stupidum*, and Chalmers expects us to believe the *stupidum*. I should be Philosopher King, so I can set things straight. I, Philosopher King, decree Chalmers's information theory of consciousness to be silly, unacceptable for contemplation, investigation, debate. Banish from your thoughts, My People!

Backpack on, over both shoulders. I used to sling it over my right shoulder, easier to get on and off. Then pinched a radial nerve, like an ice pick stabbing my shoulder, for weeks, months. Gradually recovered, self-repaired. Slip feet into Vans beside front door, another Emily choice, to replace smelly old running shoes. Emily my personal anti-entropy force, helping me resist the Second Law, delay Heat Death, descent into disorder and decay, by getting me to wear groovy shoes, jeans with rolled up cuffs.

Can win battles, not the war. Entropy gets us in the end. Cosmos expanding faster and faster, getting colder and colder, emptier and emptier. Eventually stars will wink out one by one, swallowed by their own gravity, like the Vacuum Monster in *Yellow Submarine*, sucking up everything around it, finally itself. Nothing left. But once there's something, there can't be nothing, right? The ultimate Conservation Law. I hope it's true.

Chapter 2

Commuting from Cold Spring to Hoboken

Step out of my apartment building and face the first moral quandary of the day: Stay on asphalt path or cut across grass to save time? If all residents walked on the grass, the lawn would look shitty. I should sacrifice my self-interest for the benefit of the grass, and my neighbors. Tragedy of the lawn, we must learn to be less selfish or we're fucked. Watch says 6:20. Train in 13 minutes, need to hustle to get a newspaper. I cut across the grass.

Two strips of orange crepe paper crisscross the violet predawn sky. Clouds mess up climate change forecasts, because no one knows if they'll boost or dampen warming. Someone just sent me an article on the cloud problem that quoted the old Joni Mitchell lyric: I really don't know clouds at all. I quoted that lyric when I wrote about the cloud problem 20 years ago. Green science journalism, recycling clichés.

Walk down Fair Street past humble, honest working-class houses, brick and wood with a few gingerbread flourishes. Empty trash cans and recycling bins line the sidewalk. Garbage Men already picked up the garbage, predawn, pre-traffic. Result of rational social planning. Who takes out the Garbage Man's garbage? He does, or other Garbage Men. Sensible, practical people solve logical paradoxes that stump idiot-savant philosophers.

Pass Our Lady of Loretto Church. Two stone angels, kneeling with ecstatic expressions, flank the church's entrance. I should go inside someday. Nope, never will, reminds me of the gloomy old church Mom and Dad took us to. The 9 a.m. service for kids was especially hellish. Kids sat in front, parents in back, as the mean old red-faced priest stalked the center aisle, stabbing his stumpy finger at terrified children and shouting, You! What's the Seventh Commandment! I slumped down hoping the old bastard wouldn't call on me. Never did, thank God.

Who was Our Lady of Loretto? Maybe a mystic like Teresa, skewered by the shafts of Christ's love. Brain scans show similar neural activity during orgasms and mystical visions. Mystical experiences could be a spandrel, Newberg says, side effect of sexual function. I gave a talk on science and religion at a Catholic university, and as I described the orgasm theory of religious experience, I locked eyes with a nun in the audience. I felt shame, blood rushing to my face. And pleasure. Getting away with something.

One day optogenetic implants might deliver orgasmic mystical illumination on demand. Fine, but if we're all blissed out, who will cook the food? Take out the garbage? Operate the trains? Robots, of course. And who will take care of the robots? Other robots, duh.

Enter Cup-o-cino café. *Times* already sold out. Just as well, who needs news? Always the same depressing shit. Rich getting richer, poor poorer, Republicans and Democrats squabbling, drones incinerating people in lands far, far away. Now and then something good happens. The Cold War ends, Americans elect a Black President, gays get to marry. Upticks on the long, slow path to Heat Death.

Stride down Main Street toward the train station with other commuters. Dozens of us headed toward a common destination, everyone looking straight ahead, no one speaking. Creepy, like the scene in *Time Machine*, dopey flower children in the distant future filing into a sphinx-shaped temple in silent obedient response to siren. What were they called? Eloi. We're automatons too, but at least we're not doomed to be eaten by subterranean cannibals, except maybe metaphorically.

Bottom of Main, hustle up wheelchair ramp to northbound platform. Sign by the elevator door says, Elevator to Track 1, Croton-Harmon, New York. Raised dots beneath words. Braille sign and wheelchair ramp show we take care of disabled. So did our ancestors, well before civilization began. Skeletons prove Stone Agers cared for people with broken bones and severe arthritis. The roots of goodness run deep. Just before the elevator door slides shut, I hear footsteps. Should I hold the elevator door for my fellow commuter? No, not in the mood for chitchat.

Walk to the front of the platform to be at the front of the train. Timesaver. Stand near cluster of other people talking softly. Rarely see anyone I know here. Good, too early to talk. Wait, there's Tom, a hockey buddy. He looks strange here wearing a suit, not chugging across Lake Alice in his helmet and ratty black-and-yellow sweatshirt. Quiet, not chatty. His sons play hockey with us too. Good boys.

"Hey man." "Hey, howya doing." "Okay. Can't wait for hockey." "Yeah. Won't be long now." "Have a good one." "You too."

Manly nonaggressive exchange. Cavemen did this too. They weren't all preemptively bashing each other, like Pinker and Wrangham say. Actually Tom can get pretty crazy on the ice, I'd rather play with him than against him.

Sit on the platform bench. Chilled concrete sucks heat from ass, Second Law in action. How does nature always know what to do? Every instant nature carries out infinite calculations without ever making mistakes.

Unless we were a mistake.

A honking comes across the sky, a wedge of geese hurtling over us frantically flapping. Why do they honk? Why not save their breath? Maybe exulting in shared adventure, radiant sky, sun's imminence. Why do we Ooh and Ahh over sunrises, sunsets, mountains, oceans? Instinctive love of nature? Biophilia? We hack down forests, bulldoze meadows, blow up mountains, poison rivers, but things might be worse if we lacked biophilia. Does this beauty, and our response to it, mean God exists? Even Weinberg thinks nature is more beautiful than strictly necessary.

Weinberg was so solemn when I met him in his Texas office, telling me why he can't believe in the Bible's loving, all-powerful God. Why did God let Nazis kill so many of his relatives? Because God gave us Free Will, the power to choose between good and evil? Six million Jews had to die so Nazis could exercise their Free Will? Seems like a raw deal for the Jews. And what about kids with cancer? Do cancer cells have Free Will?

Sunrise any moment. When I look at the sky, I think of other things, and stop seeing the sky. I wish I could just see the sky now and then. Really see it. Pay Attention. The tracks rumble and gleam, and the Metro North train thrums around the bend, headlight ablaze. Freud said dream trains symbolize death. Will I be ready when the train comes for me?

I wonder if aging men think more about death and less about sex. Should be testable. Give men an app that asks throughout the day if they're thinking about sex or death. No, won't work, because men will think about sex and death as soon as they see the query. Have to give men brain sensors, EEG caps or implants, that record thoughts automatically. Then sift through neural noise to find signals of dread and desire. Not an easy task, dread and desire often entangled.

As my marriage decayed, I thought about sex obsessively, uncontrollably. Too afraid to look at porn on my laptop, imagined a blowjob video popping up during classroom presentation. Bought *Penthouse* at a kiosk near Grand Central, hid it in a sock drawer at home. Discovered that after repeated viewing, images of female genitalia become asexual, like repeating a word over and over until it loses meaning. Duh. Then I met Emily, who loved me, loved sex, made me happy. And I dumped her, hurt her. Things never quite the same after she took me back.

Lots of open seats on the train. I sit in an aisle seat close to the door, so I can get out fast at Grand Central. Timesaver. Someone behind me rasps. Oh no, a snorer! Another strangled snort, then silence. Phew. Snorers can't help snoring, and I can't help hating them. They look so stupid and loathsome with their gaping fish mouths. Emily says I snore sometimes, sleeping on my back.

She doesn't mind, thinks it's cute. Nudges me if I'm too loud, tells me to roll over. True love. Why did I dump her? I still don't know.

Pay Attention. Take notebook and pen from backpack. Mind as blank as the page. Except it isn't, more like a quantum vacuum, never blank, never empty, thoughts always popping into and out of existence. Like this thought. And this one. If your mind is really empty, you're dead.

That CUNY philosopher I met in Tucson, Bob, claimed he felt emptiness all the time. Learned TM in college, and after a few years he experienced pure consciousness, no subject or object, like an eyeball seeing everything, including itself. Decided he'd reached enlightenment, goal of monks, yogis, bankers. Being enlightened is great, but it didn't change him as much as he expected. He was still a neurotic, underpaid professor living in the burbs with an unappreciative wife and kids. I thought, If this guy can be enlightened, maybe I can be too, but what's the point if you're the same old schmuck?

I wonder what Buddha would think about if he was on this train. He wouldn't be annoyed by snorers, coughers, drones anxiously swiping smartphones. No, he'd feel sorry for them, and glad he's enlightened. It would be nice to feel so superior.

Weightlifting Conductor enters the car, biceps bulging out of his blue, short-sleeved shirt. His biceps decorative, not functional, unless attracting women counts as a function. Which it does. The only function that really matters, Evo Psychos say. I hand him my ten-ride ticket. He punches it, nods, I nod back. Minimal, no frills. Actually, nods are frills, signs of mutual respect. We are not just instruments, means to each other's ends. We possess intrinsic dignity and value. All humans do. Except snorers.

The train pulls into Garrison, and I look across the Hudson at the mighty fortress of West Point, veiled in morning mist. So weird, anachronistic, like a set from *Lord of the Rings*. Its function is anachronistic too, or should be. Young men, and women now, learning to kill with guns, rockets, drones. West Point's war museum shows weapons evolving from spears, muskets and machine guns up to the bombs we dropped on Japan. Fat Man, Little Boy. Devices for mass murder, and we give them cute nicknames. When I took Neal to the war museum, we Oohed and Ahhed over the Italian machine guns. Gleaming polished works of art. Terrible things can be beautiful. A plaque over the museum's entrance says, Only the dead have seen the end of war. Soldiers probably find the aphorism heartening, like dentists thinking, Only the dead have seen the end of cavities.

Neal thinking again about dropping out of college, enlisting in the military. I try to stay calm. I say, I know how you feel, college seemed pointless to me too when I was your age. You just have to find something you love to learn. Give it time. But why should Neal take advice from me? I'm a fuck-up, couldn't save the marriage, keep the family together.

Guy in pinstripe suit slides past me into the middle seat. How about an Excuse me, Buddy? Or, Is this seat taken? My annoyance automatic, like when someone passes me on the highway. I accelerate, as an innate competitive program kicks in. Then I think, This is stupid, and slow down. Maybe we'll stop fighting wars this way. We'll all realize, This is stupid, and we'll stop. But what happens if some jerk keeps speeding?

There's the promontory with the little gravely beach where I used to swim with Gandalf. Haven't gone running or swimming with him since I moved out of the house. Probably never will again. Neal and Claire used to bring Gandalf over to my place for dinner. He thrust his snout into my crotch, I scratched under his ears, savored his familiar doggy smell. Tricia won't let him come over anymore, says he has arthritis, climbing the stairs to my apartment isn't good for him. He's eleven years old, not much time left. I'll miss him when he's gone.

That Zen Master at Esalen said dogs have Buddha Nature. All the ladies at Esalen loved the Master, thought he was the real thing, an Enlightened Guru. I thought he was a phony windbag with a slick Buddhist schtick. But maybe he was right, maybe some dogs are bodhisattvas, like Gandalf, who loves everybody.

Gandalf and I swam together just before I moved out of the house. We ran to the promontory, jumped into the Hudson, dog-paddled around each other, Gandalf's big black hairy jaws gaping, his pink tongue lapping up water, floppy ears floating like outriggers. We looked at hawks circling above us and a northbound train racing past us, we looked at each other, both grinning, thinking the same thing: This is great, isn't it? Yeah, this is great. Glad to be here with you, Buddy. In that moment, I knew what it's like to be Gandalf. He knew what it's like to be me.

Train glides under the Bear Mountain Bridge and rounds Charles Point. The twin domes of Indian Point loom above the trees. I toured the plant with that petite blond writer, Cravens… three years ago? Four? Cravens a former anti-nuke activist who changed her mind, wrote a book about how great nukes are, clean and safe, an energy source that can save us from Global Warming. She converted me, but I had residual uneasiness. As I walked through a room filled with huge turbines, enameled surfaces gleaming, not a dust ball in sight, I had ironic thoughts. Impressive! Nuclear power must be safe if this plant is so clean and shiny!

Before my conversion Pro-Nukers were bad guys or nuts. After my conversion Pro-Nukers were sensible and data-driven, and Anti-Nukers were shrill, irrational cranks. My confirmation bias underwent a phase change. I climbed on my internet soapbox and screamed, We need nukes to save us from Global Warming, people! Then fucking Fukushima happened, the quake, tsunami, meltdown. I'm still a Pro-Nuker but without the satisfying self-righteousness.

I don't write about Global Warming much. So many journalists yakking about it already, what can I add? Maybe make it personal, talk about my fear that ponds won't freeze in the Hudson Valley anymore. Other writers fret over floods, famine, Malthusian wars. I'm worried about the end of pond hockey.

We need a Scientific Savior to invent a new energy source, clean and cheap, something that taps the quantum vacuum. Maybe one of my students will be the Savior, like Fatima, in my freshman class. She'll win a Nobel for her brilliant quantum energy breakthrough, yeah, and she'll give credit to Professor Toole, who talked about how much he loved pond hockey, inspired her to save the planet.

At Peekskill station, a svelte blonde in a blue business suit glides down the aisle. Pete's ex-wife Donna! No, can't be right, Donna moved to Florida. This is happening more and more to me lately. Things resemble other things, people resemble other people. Emily teases me for squinting at the TV and misidentifying actors. I say, Hey, that's the girl from *Girls*! The British one! Emily says, No, Mr. Magoo, that actress doesn't even look like her. Sometimes I grab my laptop and confirm my guess. Look! It *is* the actress from *Girls*! I was right you were wrong! Hoo hah! Emily pats my arm and says, Good for you, Mr. Magoo.

Ramachandran says things remind us of other things because of crosstalk between tightly packed neural circuits. That's where analogies and metaphors come from. And synesthesia. Like in high school when I smoked hash in bed, lights out, stereo on, notes from "Space Cowboy" swirling around my head like phosphorescent hummingbirds, signals jumping from auditory to visual circuits. I'm old now, brain cells thinning, no synesthesia, neural crosstalk. Things resemble other things because my vision and memory are blurring. Ramachandran so clever, lots of creative crosstalk in his brain, probably inspired his crosstalk theory.

Mr. Magoo not the worst avatar. Old, half blind but cheerful. When I'm really old everything will blur into everything else and I'll know the Oneness of All Things. People will come from far and wide to worship me, Mr. Magoo, World's Greatest Guru. I'll allow female devotees to worship me privately, if Emily is no longer in the picture.

Cruise past Sing Sing, ringed by sun-gilded turrets and razor wire. Are the inmates victims of circumstance or bad seeds? Circumstance, surely, most of them. Scientists who peddle Nazi bad-seed theory should be locked up in Guantanamo and forced to read Gould and Mead until they relent.

Tappan Zee Bridge sweeps over us. I love the name Tappan Zee, so old Dutch, Hudsonish. Dad says his mom descended from Dutch in Hudson Valley, could explain my affinity for the river. So many times I've taken this train, feeling enraged, heartbroken, fearful, and my mind settles as I gaze out at the river, barges, tugboats, sailboats, gulls and cormorants, hills and hamlets on the far bank, beneath the silent sky.

Gazing at the river now, and the marmalade-glazed Palisades, I feel... good. Calm, maybe even happy. Sometimes my mood feels like the weather, beyond my control. Gusts of dread, exuberance, melancholy, anger buffet me during the day. The same thing happens over longer periods. My inner weather is mild for a while, then an anxiety front moves in, taking days to pass. I can always find reasons for my moods, like an upcoming lecture, article deadline, spat with Emily. But these are flimsy, like the day-after explanations for stock-market dips.

My moods don't stem entirely from physical factors, genes switching on and off, neurotransmitters ebbing and surging, things I'm eating and drinking. My circumstances matter, my actions matter. When I was young, I often felt bad, because I was lonely and wasn't sure what to do with my life. Then I found meaningful work, and love, got married, had kids. My inner climate changed, my baseline mood shifted toward happiness. Shifted back to unhappiness when things with Tricia got bad.

There's some deep connection between happiness and Free Will. When you're happy, you just do what you do, not thinking too much, like riding a roller coaster. No, too passive. Like playing pond hockey, darting up the black ice toward big bad Sven thinking, I'm gonna beat you, man! Fly around him right side or left, or maybe smack the puck between his skates and watch Sven grimace as the puck clonks against the goal board. I love that wonderful musical sound, Clonk! And I yell, Yeah! Or maybe Sven jabs his mighty ten-foot-long arm out, pokes the puck away from me and over to Dick who swoops around Tim and fires at our goal board. Clonk! That hideous noise! And Sven yells, Ha! And I yell, Damn you Sven! He's won this time, altered my trajectory, frustrated me, but it doesn't matter because we've chosen the game, we love the game, we win even if we lose.

Sometimes I get frustrated when my team is getting its ass kicked. I act like an asshole, curse, yell at teammates for screwing up. Then I stop, lean on my stick, breathe deeply. Pay Attention. Look at the winter sky, hills, trees, my buddies. Remind myself, It's just a game. Chill. Be glad to be here playing, before Global Warming takes it all away.

Maybe someday science will give us power over our inner weather. Implants that deliver joy on demand, that block heartbreak and dread. No one could resist that technology. The end of suffering might also mean the end of creativity, of meaning, but no one would care. If implants malfunction, who would fix them? Robots. And no one will give a shit about Global Warming.

Sven can't play anymore. His wife brought him to a game last winter, so he could watch from the shore. I skated over and said, Hey Sven! He smiled at me uncertainly, couldn't remember who I was. Sven had a good run, lots of happiness in that man's life. Death isn't so bad if you had a good life. And if your life was hard, death's a relief.

South of Yonkers the train veers over to the Harlem River, so tame and urbanized after the mythic, majestic Hudson. Then the Harlem River disappears as the train rumbles past cement plants, warehouses, parking lots, baseball fields, under bridges, roads, ramps, and now we rise, skim on elevated track over Harlem, past basketball courts, red and beige brick buildings, cranes, scaffolding, signs of construction, growth, renewal. Pass Foot Center of New York, big blocky building in the heart of Harlem. Imagine multiethnic doctors healing the feet of grateful multiethnic patients. Decades ago Harlem had a creepy, apocalyptic *Mad Max* look. Buildings along train tracks wrapped in razor wire, defaced with graffiti, gang slang, religious rants.

Garbage piled high in alleys. Harlem's growing now, healing, rebuilding, defying entropy.

Train plunges into darkness. Almost a relief, this sensory deprivation. I once paid for a session in a sensory deprivation tank, an oversized coffin filled with salty water, the same temperature as skin, so you float, feel nothing, your body vanishes, you become Pure Consciousness in empty infinite space. I was stoned, decided to reach out to The Emptiness, talk to It. Serious, not serious. Then I felt something coming, something intelligent, powerful, coming fast toward me from deep space. A mystery, a monster. Threw open the tank door, jumped out, hyperventilating, soaking wet in the bright room, naked. Feeling like an idiot. Scaredy-Cat. I should have stayed in the tank, confronted the Mystery Monster. Because, come on, there is no Monster. Or if there is, I am the Monster. One actor plays all the parts of this crazy play. My Big Drug Trip taught me that. And *Star Wars*.

Bald guy across the aisle brays into his cell phone, "Have you talked to Rick yet? You gotta talk to Rick..." Yackety yack. Classic Cell Phone Asshole. I wait a minute, then wave at him. He ignores me. I say, loudly, "Excuse me, can you talk less loudly?" Cell Phone Asshole talks *louder*, puts his hand up, palm toward me, as if trying to mute me. Other passengers ignore me and Cell Phone Asshole, look straight ahead. No one wants to get involved.

"Can you believe that guy?" A female voice behind me. I turn. Big Blond Lady looking at me, shaking her head.

"Yeah," I say, shaking my head too. Grateful for her support.

Cell Phone Asshole stops talking. Then a baby starts squalling behind me. Big Blond Lady says, "Shush!" Another female voice says, "He's a baby! *You* shush!" Must be the baby's Mom. Big Blond Lady snorts in disgust. I can feel her eyes boring into the back of my head, demanding my support, because she supported me against Cell Phone Asshole. Reciprocal altruism. I ignore her, stare stoically forward. Big Blond Lady is unreasonable. You can't tell a baby to shush! Babies don't have Free Will.

Well before our arrival in Grand Central, the ritual of disembarkation begins, a marvel of self-organization. You can leave your seat and move toward the door while the train's still rolling. But once the train stops, you must let people in the rows ahead of you exit first. A tacit rule. After the train lurches to a stop, people exiting rows glance at people already standing in the aisle, exchanging smiles and nods. We happily choose cooperation over self-interest for our common benefit, to avoid anarchy and save time. Those who fail to follow rules are usually outsiders, kids or tourists. Even psychopathic lawyers and bankers adhere to the train's unspoken etiquette. Makes me proud to be human.

Exit train, scoot past plodders out of the tunnel and into the main chamber of Grand Central. Truly grand now, windows, marble columns, staircases scrubbed clean, not seedy and sooty like the old days. The ceiling is especially grand, emblazoned with gold stars, constellations, signs of the Zodiac. Hunter, Fish, Scorpion, Crab. The Crab is my sign and Emily's. Tiny light bulbs embedded in stars twinkle in the fake sky.

After we started dating, Emily checked our charts and told me our prospects weren't great, Cancers don't go well with Cancers. I said, How can you believe that stuff? Astrology is just a product of our overactive imaginations, our childish, narcissistic belief that the stars and planets were created for our benefit. My usual pompous rant. I remembered her prediction when I broke up with her a year later. When we got back together I said, Fuck the stars, Baby, we make our own fate.

The foot traffic in Grand Central seems chaotic, but if you plotted individuals' trajectories, patterns would emerge. People drift, shuffle, dash. Or stand, scanning departure announcements or looking for lost companions. Halfway across the terminal, I find myself on a collision course with a dasher, a chunky guy in a brown suit. We feint and juke until our chests almost bump before sliding past each other with irritated grimaces and eye rolls. Our brains are such sophisticated navigators, and yet we still end up in awkward jigs of confusion.

Universal implants would eliminate this problem. My implant, swapping signals with those of other commuters, would calculate the optimal, collision-free trajectory and command my motor cortex accordingly. Implants can't eliminate all problems. No perfect solutions to friendship, work, international relations. They are NP-hard, like the traveling salesman problem. But implants could reduce the confusion that leads to conflict. If Tricia and I had implants, maybe we'd still be married. Probably not.

Slam through swinging doors, take out wallet, extract Metro Card, swipe through turnstile slot. The turnstile instantly subtracts a fee and informs me I have $32.50 left on the card. Minor engineering marvel making life a little easier. Timesaver. Huge advance beyond '80s era of clunky subway tokens, exploited by Subway Trolls who jammed cardboard in token slots, sucked out tokens, resold them.

Waiting for the Shuttle to Times Square, I listen to a bearded old hippy on the platform sing "Light My Fire." His open guitar case littered with bills and coins. He probably primed the case with money to encourage donations, knows we are herd creatures, more likely to do what others have done. I drop a dollar into the guitar case and nod at the musician, who nods back. Tough way to make a buck. But is science blogging better? I'm begging internet surfers, Please pause a moment, read me. Actually, you don't even have to read me, just Tweet me, Like me, tell others to Like me. Might be nice having a more functional job, like subway conductor or garbage man, except robots might take their jobs away. Robots will never take my job, science blogging isn't important enough to replace.

Shuttle arrives, people get off, we get on. People in my car sit and stand, reading e-books, smartphones, newspapers, absorbing information for entertainment or self-advancement. Information must surprise you, tell you something you didn't know, change your options, or it's not information, it's just mindless physics. If information exists, so do minds, and so does Free Will.

I bet no one here is reading a science blog.

Young guy in a suit sticks his briefcase between closing doors and squeezes in, saying, "Sorry, sorry." We're all thinking, Wait for the next train, jerk, but we say nothing, because we are good, decent people. When the doors slide open in Times Square, we exit in polite, orderly fashion. Not like sheep. We are dignified, mutually respectful, rational humans following the Golden Rule in spite of impatience and irritation. Maybe a little like sheep, but in a good way. Conformity can be a force for good.

I walk along the edge of the southbound platform, monitoring people around me for unpredictable moves that could bump me onto the tracks. Would I save someone who fell on the tracks, like the Subway Samaritan? When he saw a guy having a seizure fall on the tracks, the Samaritan jumped onto him and held him down as the subway roared over them. A real hero.

Where do altruistic impulses come from? Risking your life for a stranger? Evo Psychos say natural selection bred altruism into our ancestors because good deeds were often rewarded, boosting Do Gooders' reproductive prospects. Tit for tat. Subway Samaritan got lots of tit for his tat. Bush invited him to the State of the Union, Trump wrote him a check. I admired the Subway Samaritan until I learned he had teenage daughters. What would have happened to them if he'd been killed? I'll never be a Subway Samaritan. I have kids! And I'm a coward.

Someone yelling, a woman sitting on a bench beside bulging plastic bags. "Leave me alone!" she screams. "I'm a good mother!" No one is there, she's yelling at air. Our minds teem with alter egos, but most of us can tell real personas from imaginary ones. Not schizophrenics. Their inventions come to life and torment them, like Frankenstein's monster. They hear messages in thunder, bird songs, the rustling of leaves in a tree. If schizophrenics are charismatic, they can become prophets, religious leaders like Moses, Mohammed, Sister Teresa. Or Nobel laureates like Nash, the guy with the beautiful mind. Most end up like this poor lady screaming on the subway platform. Scientists don't have a clue what schizophrenia is. They should spend less time on consciousness and more on schizophrenia.

On the PATH, careening under the Hudson to Hoboken, I brood over how often I've done this before. Week after week I commute to Hoboken to teach the same students. Next semester I start over with a fresh crop. I get older, grayer, more wrinkled. But I'm becoming a better teacher, if only because I was so bad to begin with. Life's okay, as long as we can achieve a few temporary triumphs over entropy.

Kauffman suspects there's a creative force countering the Second Law, generating order from disorder, turning cosmic dust and debris into stars, planets, amoebas and humans, who create writing, math, science. McKenna proposed a Novelty-Generating Force countering disorder at all scales, from personal to global. Novelty can be good or bad, the internet or the H-bomb, Gandhi or Hitler, but it keeps the plot moving, surprises us, makes us say, Holy Shit! Wow! Awesome! The Acid Head's version of a Divine Plan.

McKenna a real joker, liked goofing on people, but his novelty theory isn't goofier than any other theology or theory of everything. He laid it all out for me in '99 over lunch on the top floor of the Millennium Hotel, right across from the Twin Towers, which were still standing. He said we were headed for a surprise, didn't know what it was, but it was going to be big. A brain tumor killed him less than a year later. That was a surprise. And he just missed the big surprise of 9/11.

Emily is my personal anti-entropy force. She took a banged-up divorced guy, hammered out the dents, dabbed on fresh paint. Almost good as new! Just don't look too closely.

Exit Hoboken terminal, bear right across the cobblestone parking lot to the Hudson promenade. Men and women hustle north and south on the promenade carrying shoulder bags, briefcases, backpacks. Dark-skinned women push light-skinned children in carriages. A sleek young man wearing earbuds

strides past me, yelling, hands slicing the air, eyes focused
on an invisible person before him. Not schizophrenic, just
a typical Smartphone Junkie. More and more we're digitally
connected, texting, phoning, emailing each other. Preview of the
Singularity, ultimate mind meld, when we all become one.

Singularity nuts better hope the mind meld fantasy doesn't
come true. You need at least two things for there to be
something. You need a mind, and something else. If everything
is one thing, that's the same as nothing. Same with Buddhists
hoping we all become one.

A lovely, sunny morning, but no one seems to care. Everyone is
on a mission, rushing somewhere. Where? Remember talk by
that adjunct art professor, Elsa, sleeveless shirt showing off her
pale arms and shoulders, laced with blue veins. She showed us
slides of paintings, black, bloody canvases with slits in them
like tears in spacetime. Or cosmic vaginas. She came up with
the idea for her best work when she was in an airport, on an
escalator, and a guy jabbering on a phone pushed past her. Elsa
yelled after him, Rushing to your death? She didn't know where
the question came from, it just popped out of her mouth. The
guy looked back at her, freaked out. She got a grant to rent a
billboard on a Jersey highway that asked commuters, Rushing to
Your Death?

I'm rushing to my death. But what's the alternative? Dawdling,
lollygagging toward death? Yeah, maybe. Stop, slow down,
lollygag. Pay Attention. Don't dwell on death too much.
Wouldn't it be ironic if a driver distracted by the billboard
crashed and died?

Blue, white, yellow ferries churn up, down, across the shining
Hudson. Beyond the river, the Empire State Building guards a

flock of lesser buildings. Another skyscraper looks like a giant plucked it from its foundation, dipped its tip in molten gold and set it right-side up again. As I walk along the river, the apparent distance between skyscrapers shifts. Parallax effect. We can't see distances between stars shift as the Earth swings around the Sun because stars are so far, far away. We are infinitesimal, compared to the cosmos, but we matter.

Before I veer off the promenade toward school, I pass a gray-haired woman in a red tracksuit. She's not rushing to her death. She is standing still beside the river, arms raised, looking at the sky, beaming. Paying Attention.

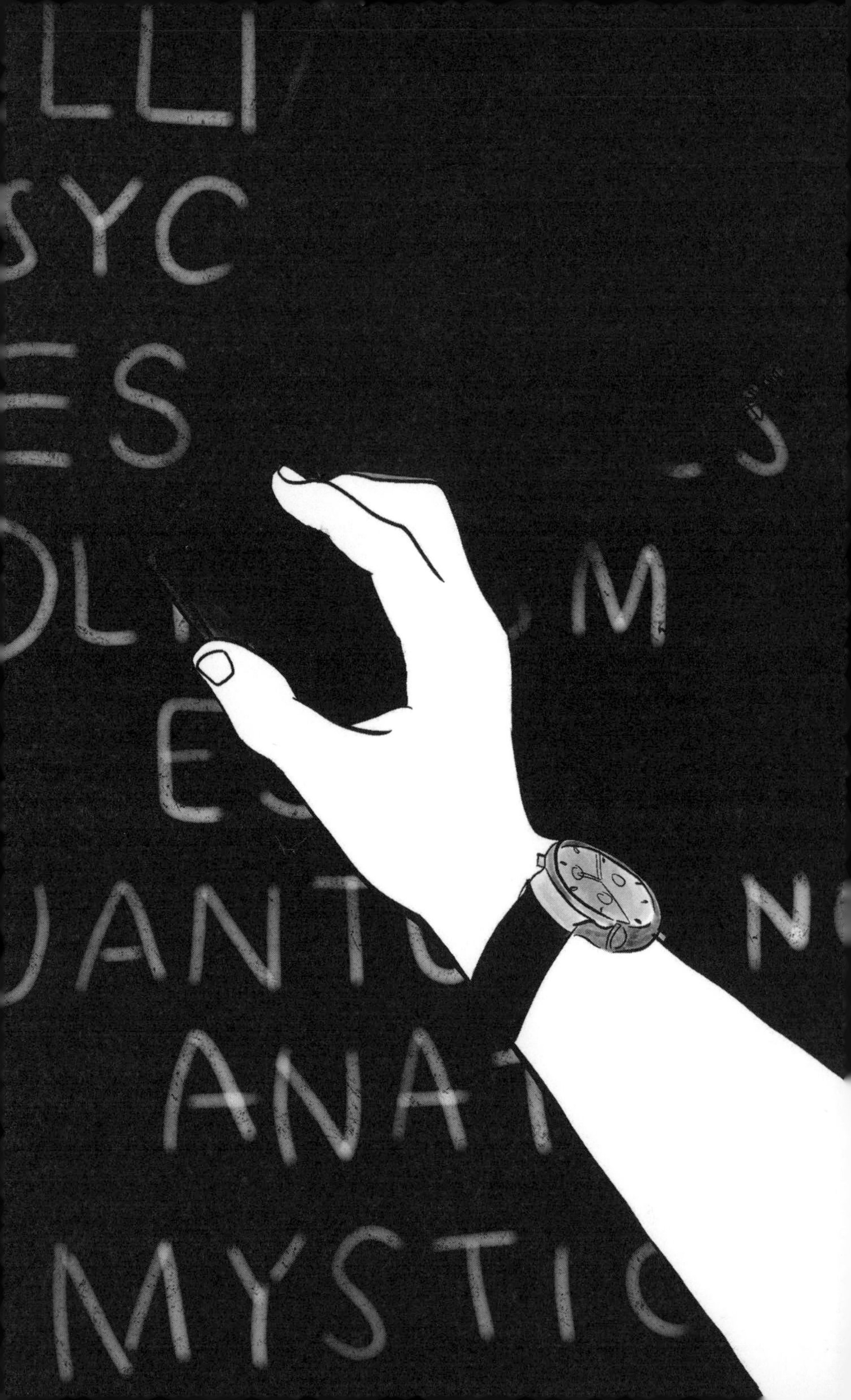

Chapter 3

Teaching a Freshman Humanities Seminar

Enter Humanities Center lobby, flat-screen TV playing a loop of Humanities Dean extolling Philosophy, History, Literature, Art and Music, Social Science. And Science Communication, my program. Giving students skills to become journalists, attack Evil Doers, Big Pharma, Big Oil, Military Industrial Complex. Or skills to work for Evil Doers. More jobs, better money.

Drain bladder in second-floor bathroom, climb stairs to third floor. Approaching room 307, take keys from pocket to open door without pausing. Saving time, rushing to my death. Unload backpack, sit in swivel chair, open notebook. Pay Attention. On my desk a photo of beaming Emily stands beside a bronze brontosaurus, memento from our first year, when she still gave me little sciencey gifts, called me Science Man, before switching to Mr. Magoo. Photo of me with Neal and Claire. Neal looks cool, skeptical. Claire smiles drowsily, eyes half-lidded. My mysterious offspring, bearers of my genes.

No more propagating genes for me. Three months after meeting Emily, I went to a clinic in Katonah, where a pretty blond nurse injected me with an anesthetic and shaved me as I stared at the ceiling, too cowardly to make eye contact. I closed my eyes as the Doc moved in. After a few tugs and yanks, he announced he was done. So quick and painless! Later, when the anesthetic wore off, I felt like someone kicked me. Emily horrified when I showed her my black and blue balls. She caressed me, whispering, Poor Monkey Man. I begged her not to stop, and we did it, gingerly, two days earlier than the Doc advised. Everything still worked! The vasectomy is a genuine medical advance, tiny risk and huge benefit, unlike tests and treatments for cancer. Who got the first vasectomy? A brave man. Or a prisoner, a mental patient, some poor schmuck with no choice.

9:14, plenty of time before class. Check email. Message from Emily, finally! No words, just a link to video of an elephant and chihuahua hanging out. Is that us? She loves stories about different species bonding, even predators and prey, like a lion and meerkat. She wants me to write about why this happens. Too cute, I say, I do serious stuff. Bullshit answer, I write about lots of silly stuff. Multiverses, Singularity, God.

Finally did a story she wanted me to, about a cat whose engineer-owner hung a camera around its neck. Cat Cam. Automatically snapped photos as the cat wandered around its neighborhood. Haunting ground-level shots of empty lonely suburban streets, drainage pipes, another cat crouched under a car. I wrote it up with the headline, What Is It Like To Be a Cat? Readers loved it. Of course, Emily said, You finally wrote something interesting.

She gets upset if I don't look at stuff she sends. I reply to the elephant-chihuahua link, *Funny! See u tonite baby!* Cut

42

unnecessary letters to save time, project playful informality. Don't send yet. *Funny* implies I watched the elephant-chihuahua video. It's 11 minutes, too long. Do little white lies matter? My utilitarian practical self thinks, Nah, no big deal. My goody-goody Superego thinks, Little lies make big lies easier. And do you really want another relationship built on lies and evasions? Substitute *Thanks!* for *Funny!* Send email, feeling virtuous.

What time is it? 9:42, 18 minutes to go. Waiting for class to begin does funny things to time perception. I think: Plenty of time, plenty of time, still plenty... No time! Instantaneous phase transition from calm to panicky. Happens on longer time scales too. When exactly do you stop being young? Become old? Impossible to pinpoint the transition, but it happens. Like Zeno's paradox. Getting from here to there takes infinite steps. So how can you possibly ever arrive? Get old? Become that grizzled guy in the mirror? It happens. It happened to me. Our finite lives compounded of infinitesimals, unless string theorists are right and strings are the smallest things, the Ground of Being. There must be a Ground of Being, or we'd tumble down, down, down into a vortex of infinite smallness.

Lay out teaching equipment on my desk. Markers, pen, notes on James. Put everything in backpack. Extra markers in case one or two are dry. Redundancy inefficient, but sometimes necessary to avoid disasters. Oh, don't forget the digital recorder. Take a leak again? Get a drink of water? Still jittery before class after all these years. Stage fright once my secret shame, like a demon punishing me for the desire to pontificate. When I first got speaking invitations, I did push-ups and vodka shots beforehand. Also tried deep breathing, saying Duh. And imagining the audience dead, me dead, nothing matters, especially not this stupid talk. That just added melancholy to anxiety.

Stage fright from nature or nurture? I had a primal stage trauma in fourth grade, new kid in school, homeroom teacher picked me for a big spelling bee. Sat on stage before hundreds of students and teachers. I went first, spelled P-U-M-K-I-N. The teacher on stage said mournfully, I'm sorry, Eamon. Frowns, smiles, whispers in the audience. My homeroom teacher looked stricken. I had to sit on stage until the bee was over, an eternity. Does that trauma explain my stage fright? Probably not, too simple. Must be biological too. Stage fright so mysterious. Do people with autism have it? Schizophrenia? What about sociopaths, or supposedly enlightened gurus? Is it a modern disorder? Like anorexia? Or ancient? Testable. Observe Kalahari hunters, see if any panic when buddies say, Hey tell everyone how that elephant almost stomped you this morning!

Stage fright reveals something about the self, how we shuttle between inner and outer worlds, maintain ourselves as avatars. We all deep down feel like imposters, terrified of being exposed, naked, under the spotlight of others' attention. We feel like imposters because we are imposters. Figments of our own imaginations. I felt like an imposter when I began teaching, especially the Humanities Seminar. I'm a science writer, not a professor! Teaching got easier, then hard again as my marriage fell apart. I perceived students dimly, heard myself droning about Plato's cave while tormenting myself with questions: Why doesn't she love me? Can I make her love me again? Should I stay or leave? What will happen to Neal and Claire? Teaching is much less stressful now, after eight years. We're creatures of habit. Fears, desires seem permanent until experience erodes them, making way for new fears and desires.

9:58! No-time-left-I'm-late!

Grab backpack, exit office, trot down stairs, cross the street into Althofer. Three of my students wait for the elevator. Good Lacrosse Guy, Scraggly Beard and Bad Lacrosse Guy, that smartass punk. What are their names? No idea. Halfway through the semester and I only know a few names. I'm such a shitty teacher. Hope I don't overhear them saying something snide about me. We want to know, don't want to know, what others think of us. There will be no more secrets after the Singularity, cyber version of Judgment Day.

"Gentlemen," I say. They turn. "Hi Professor," etc. My first year teaching, I told students they could call me Eamon. Few did. Don't offer the option now. Formality, respect for authority not so bad. We're not equals. I'm not wise, but I'm wiser than them. Wisdom is like Free Will, a relative not absolute trait.

Elevator arrives, we shuffle in, accelerate up five floors. "Nice day, huh?" I say. "Yeah," they nod. "That humidity last week was killing me," I say. Yes, they agree, humidity was awful.

Enter classroom, filled with students clustered, chattering. Stumble over coiled power cord near the podium. That was close! Someone guffaws, back of the room, probably Bad Lacrosse Guy. You think that's funny? See how funny it is when I fail your ass. That's what I should say, but I'm too nice, too chickenshit. Wish I could unleash my inner sociopath. Face burning, with rage or embarrassment?

Settle behind the podium, take notes, markers, pen, recorder out of backpack. Breathe in, breathe out. Face still warm, I know they can see it, makes it warmer. James guessed physiological symptoms come first, trigger subjective conscious emotion. His theory is too simple. Blushing leads to feeling of embarrassment, leads to more blushing. Nasty feedback effect.

Do boners lead to subjective feeling of horniness, or vice versa? Face still red? Hell with it, I am Alpha Male, Silverback Gorilla. Hear me thump my chest and bellow! Remember recorder, Pay Attention Project. Do I want to do this? Do I need to tell them?

"I'm going to be doing something a little weird today. I mean, weirder than usual. Unless anyone objects, I'd like to record today's class with this digital recorder. It's for a writing project. If I end up publishing anything based on this recording, I'll change your names. Does anyone have any objections?"

Silence. Like they would give a shit. Kids post photos of themselves drunk, half-naked on Facebook. Maybe not these kids, but Kids. Why should they care if an Old Fart like me writes boring stuff about this boring class? And if I can't remember their names now, I probably won't remember when I transcribe this recording. "No? Good. Then here goes." Press RECORD, confirm red light on, put recorder on podium. "Okay, ready for William James?" Back of the room, someone with head down, eyes closed. Sleeping! Already! Nose Ring Girl. Should wake up sleepers, shame them, but never do. Chickenshit.

Grab marker, turn to whiteboard, write: WILLIAM JAMES: 1842-1910. Writing on whiteboard for me not them, vents nervous energy, keep hands busy. "James came from a really distinguished family. His brother was Henry James, the novelist. Have any of you read Henry James? No? Have any of you *heard* of Henry James? Okay, a few of you, that's good. Anyway, the James brothers came from this family of high achievers, who had pretty serious psychological problems. William James struggled with depression and panic attacks for most of his life. He was always searching for something that could save him from his demons. That gave his writings on psychology an emotional intensity that you don't often see in science. Which maybe you noticed in the reading for today." Lucky for us the poor bastard never found salvation.

Write PSYCHOLOGY on the board. "Also, just to provide some context for our discussion, let me remind you that we're talking about psychology in a Humanities class. Right? Along with history, literature and philosophy. Why isn't psychology taught in the science department along with physics and chemistry? Maybe as we talk about James we can also talk about the field of psychology and how it has progressed—or not progressed— over the last century." Pause, scan the room. "So what are your thoughts about James's thoughts about thoughts?" Fatima smiles, I silently thank her. All I want is a little appreciation, especially from smart kids like Fatima.

Bad Lacrosse Guy thrusts his hand up first as usual. He keeps missing classes, handing in papers late, crappy papers. Thinks he can make up for it by blabbing when he's here. "I thought it was interesting, the whole part where he talks about how..." Bad Lacrosse Guy pauses, making it up as he goes, probably skimmed the reading right before class. "You can't think what someone else thinks. Because, like, in general your life makes you think the way you do. So no one else can think the way you do. It's kind of, like, individuality."

"Mmm hmm," I say. I won't honor him with a follow-up remark. Good Lacrosse Guy lifts his hand. I smile, nod at him.

Good Lacrosse Guy: "James reminds me a little of Descartes? Because they both focus so much on thinking? Like when he says, I think therefore I am? But I wanted to ask you, did James worry that the world is a figment of our imagination, the way Descartes did?"

Kiss-ass but a good one, knows how to play the game. He'll get a good grade. "That's a really good comparison," I say, writing DESCARTES on the board. "As far as I know James never worried, the way Descartes did, that reality is really an illusion created by evil demons, like in *The Matrix*. But they definitely share some of the same obsessions."

Good Lacrosse Guy: "Also, I liked James's writing style. It was easy to follow along, but it was also scientific. It explained things, and gave good examples, and talked about peoples' research. I like him a lot more than Descartes and most of the other people we've had to read so far."

"I'm glad you brought up his writing style," I say. "James is one of my all-time favorite writers. I read him for pleasure as well as for insight and information. The irony is that James agonized over how inadequate words are for describing all the things that go on in our heads. He pointed out that lots of our thoughts can't be put into words, and we distort them when we try." Hold hands up, thumbs out, framing my head. Roll eyes upward as if trying to see into my own brain. "Okay, now I'm going to look at a thought in my head. What does that even mean? James says it's like trying to study snowflakes by capturing them in your hand. As soon as you capture the snowflake, it starts to melt. As soon as you pay attention to a thought..." I clench my fists and flick my fingers out like a magician. "Poof! It's gone."

Is that true? What about this thought in my head right now? Can't I think it and observe it? Put it into words? Sure. But while I observe it, Pay Attention to it, express it, I'm missing all the other thoughts swarming around it. And what about all the thoughts I don't let myself think? Remember that thing Wittgenstein said: If a lion could talk, we couldn't understand it. Yeah, and if our subconscious could talk, we couldn't understand it either, it would just be grunts and growls. That's good. Tell them, so it's on the recorder? No, stick with James, but remember, remember, write it down later.

Bad Lacrosse Guy jabbering again. "Sorry," I say, "I didn't catch that, could you…" Bad Lacrosse Guy shakes his head and waves his hand, telling me to move on. Good. But what was I saying? Wait, James, the subconscious… Oh yeah! "James also has a great metaphor for trying to understand subconscious thoughts. He compares it to studying darkness by shining a light into it. But James's brilliance as a writer brings me back to the question of whether psychology is really a science. If we value a scientist primarily because of his verbal skill, is he really a scientist? Or is he more of a literary figure, like Shakespeare?"

Bad Lacrosse Guy: "Also I think that…"

"Hold on!" I say. "Leave something for other people to talk about." Giggles. Bad Lacrosse Guy looks annoyed. Good.

Mick in a monotonic robot voice: "I like when James talks about consciousness being sensibly continuous. It's like when you black out. The moments before you blacked out and the moments after just flow together, like a river or stream. It feels like one whole, continuous thing." Damn. Referring to his own blackout experiences? Mick told me after missing the first paper deadline that he's depressed, having a hard time caring about school. Report him to school psychologist? Cover my ass?

Pony Tail Girl with usual brisk confidence: "One thing I liked was when James was talking about how physical things don't change, but our feelings do. So you're always playing the same piano, but the feeling you have each time you play is different. Or you look at the grass, and it's physically the same, but it will look different in daytime and nighttime. So although it's the same thing you're looking at, your thoughts will always vary."

"Yes, exactly," I say. "What's the title of this piece by James again? Stream of Thought, right? That's a great metaphor to help us grasp how fluid our thoughts are. They're always moving and changing. They never stay still."

Pony Tail Girl: "Also I like what James said about art. If you try to describe color to a blind person, you say, I feel like the color blue is calming. But someone else might feel something different about blue. So your sensation of something will not always be the same as someone else's."

"Right," I reply, "and here's the thing. I can try to tell you how the world looks to me, and you can tell me how it looks to you. But our words can't really capture our experiences. No one really knows what it is like to be anyone else. In fact, I can't be sure any of you is experiencing anything at all. Remember when I talked about solipsism last week? This is what I meant. Sometimes I think life comes down to trying to solve the solipsism problem. We're all trapped inside our own little subjective worlds. We're lonely, and we're desperate to get out. Love can make us feel like we've escaped ourselves, but we never do, really." They stare at me. Too much?

Bad Lacrosse Guy, sitting next to Pony Tail Girl, whispers something in her ear. He smirks, she smiles slightly. Hope they're not a couple. She's too good for him, too sensible, hard-working, pretty. She should forget Bad Lacrosse Guy, hang out with Good Lacrosse Guy. Hope she's not a Girl Who Likes Bad Boys.

Dragon Tattoo lifts his hand. So brave! He opens his mouth: "I I I…" He pauses, composes himself. I beam encouragement at him. He always has something smart to say, if he can get it out. Does his stutter cause stage fright or vice versa? Does the stutter come from a primal trauma? A genetic neurochemical glitch? "I th-th-think a lot of the things we d-d-do, we think in similar ways," Dragon Tattoo says. "For example, a lot of artists are going to agree about what color goes with another color in a painting. Also if you go into a c-c-court with lawyers debating in front of a jury, they are usually going to reach the same conclusion because of the evidence provided, and say, This p-p-person is guilty."

I can feel my mirror neurons pinging. Must repress empathy, or I'll stutter too. "Okay, let me see if I understand what you're saying. The hope of philosophers going back to Plato and Aristotle is that reason and observation should lead us to the same conclusions about reality. Is that what you're suggesting?"

Dragon Tattoo: "Yeah. Like if… if… if you're doing math. If y-y-you write 1 + 1 on the board, everyone will think 2. And everyone accepts the P-P-Pythagorean Theorem. Or accepts that a circle's circumference is p-p-pi times the diameter. And ph-ph-physicists agree on how atoms work, or the structure of molecules."

"This is really important," I say. "How universal is reason? Sometimes reason leads all of us, or most of us, in the same direction. It overcomes the differences in our subjective perceptions. But often it doesn't. When it comes to things like religion, and morality, and government policies—and even science!—smart, rational people can look at the same data and reach different conclusions." Yeah, think of all the brainiacs who believe in crap like the Singularity, strings, multiverses. I alone am truly rational.

Pony Tail Girl: "I was thinking about whether psychology is a science or not. I think one problem with psychology is that different people react so differently to the same stimuli. So two people can grow up in the same circumstances, and one will be suicidal and the other will be optimistic and successful. So over here you have studies that say, 'This is how these people think and act.' But that's not true if you look at other people."

"Another good point," I say. "Just think about how hard psychology is compared to physics. If you understand one electron, you understand every single electron in the universe, right? And you understand electrons a billion years ago and a billion years into the future, as far as we know. But every single human who has ever been born is different from every other human. And not only that. You"—I jab my finger at Pony Tail Girl—"are different right now than you were before this class! James pointed out these problems, but he didn't say, Let's throw up our hands and give up. He was saying, We have to come to grips with this."

Plane hum wafts through window. Louder louder, softer softer.

Hand up. Nose Ring Girl. She's aliiiiiiiiiive!

"So you mentioned whether psychology is a science?" she says in a sleepy voice. "And whether psychology has really evolved since James was writing? I think one of the main ways is how we diagnose people? And the way psychologists go about treating them? In James's time, if someone had multiple personality disorder or something, people would say, You're, like, possessed by the Devil. Or, like, You're crazy, let's throw you in prison. And there are much better medicines now?"

"Actually," I say, "our treatments for mental illness haven't progressed that much over the last 100 years. All the supposedly amazing drugs we have for schizophrenia, depression and other mental disorders don't work that well. And neither do all our modern psychotherapies." Nose Ring Girl and others look baffled, suspicious. Probably some are on meds for depression, anxiety, attention deficit, whatever. An inner voice harangues me: Who the hell do you think you are! Standing in front of vulnerable young people spouting cranky anti-medical crap. The gall! You have no right! No authority! That voice was insistent when I started teaching, but now it's faint, easy to reject. I, Professor Eamon Toole, am in charge! I have authority!

Scraggly Beard, scowling, shifting in his seat, thrusts a hand up. "When James says no one can think what you think, that's not entirely true. I have a couple of friends back home who are twins. One is a girl, one is a guy. And if one is in danger, the other one will almost, like"—he snaps his fingers—"have this... hint, and know something is wrong."

Oh no. Do I want to deal with this? "Yeah, you're talking about extrasensory perception. ESP."

Scraggly Beard: "Yeah! That's what they call it!"

"According to the vast majority of scientists," I say, "ESP isn't real, but a lot of people believe in it. You mentioned a classic example. You're tossing and turning in bed, and suddenly you have this vision of a friend or relative in trouble. And then you get a phone call and find out that person was in a car crash. How many of you think that happens? Or have had an experience like that yourself?" Thirteen, fourteen. More than half the class. Some don't raise hands, maybe because they think I'll disapprove, or they just don't care.

Pony Tail Girl: "I think a lot of these ESP-type experiences are really based on subconscious clues that we pick up. Because a lot of times, with me and my brother, I'll be at the kitchen table or something, and he'll come in singing the same song I was singing a couple of minutes ago. And we'll go, That's really strange. But it could have been that earlier in the day he was singing the song, and I heard him, and it got in my head."

"Yes!" I say. "That's how a good scientist thinks. If you're a scientist, you go through all the boring, common-sense explanations before you consider the cool, far-out explanations. For example, when you're thinking about someone and get the phone call about them or whatever, it's natural to remember that coincidence and come up with a causal theory for it, because that's what our big brains do. You don't remember all the other times when you're thinking about someone and you don't get the phone call."

Scraggly Beard: "But could there maybe be, like, some kind of signals that our brains are using to communicate with each other? Like some kind of electromagnetic waves that science hasn't discovered yet?"

"Okay," I say, "we're getting off topic, but what the hell. There is something in quantum mechanics that some people think could explain ESP. It's called quantum nonlocality, or spooky action at a distance." Giggles. "Seriously. Einstein called it spooky action at a distance to make fun of it, he didn't believe in it, it was too weird. The basic idea is, you have two particles, like photons, particles of light, that are produced by the same source and then fly apart. If you do something to this photon over here, like detect it with an instrument, you affect the other photon instantly, even if it's light years away. It makes absolutely no sense according to ordinary physics, but it's been confirmed

experimentally. Spooky action"—raise hands, curl forefingers—
"is real."

Scraggly Beard: "So why can't that explain why there's this ESP
connection between humans? Between, like, twins and other
people?"

"Some scientists think that's possible," I say. "But for spooky
action to happen, particles have to be totally isolated in a
vacuum or under very cold conditions, near absolute zero. As
soon as you get into something warm and squishy, like a human
brain, all the spooky quantum effects wash out."

Scraggly Beard: "Yeah, but, like, there are so many things in the
universe that we don't understand yet. So maybe ESP is real. I'm
just saying, like, the whole universe blows your mind."

You're telling me, Scraggly. Should I tell him my ghost story?
Sipping cocktails with Tricia in that old farmhouse in Maine,
and we heard sobbing. A woman, upstairs, crying. Hairs on the
back of my neck actually stood up. Tricia and her roommate
laughed, watching me. They had heard Crying Ghost Lady
before, and had told me about her, but I didn't believe them.
When I went upstairs, the crying stopped. No one was there.
Still can't explain Crying Ghost Lady. An anomaly. Not enough
to abandon my skepticism and get all flaky, New Agey, but still.
Emily says her best decisions come from Intuition. Does she
believe in ESP? I should ask her.

"William James was open-minded about ESP," I say. "And
I know some big shot modern scientists who believe in it.
I don't believe in ESP, because I haven't seen good evidence
for it. I wish there was! If we found solid evidence for ESP, that
would be so cool! It would blow science wide open! But there

is nothing. Yet." Pause. "That's enough about ESP. What other reactions do you have to James?"

Bad Lacrosse Guy: "I was really interested in what James said about subconscious selves, because I have had experience of that. Like last year, when I was trying to decide where to go to college. My parents wanted me to go to this Catholic college. But something told me I should come here. It felt like the decision was kind of made for me, by, like, some kind of subconscious force. And it made the right decision for me, because I really like it here."

Brilliant insight, thanks for sharing. "Umm, yeah. All of us occasionally do things because of a hunch, or intuition, which we can't really explain. Also, any of you who have struggled with, like, smoking cigarettes, or eating junk food, you know how divided your self can be. One part of you is saying, Don't do that, that's bad. It's trying to control this other self in you that's doing the bad thing. Your selves are fighting with each other!"

Mick's hand goes up: "I feel like the subconscious is who you really are." Flat tone, deadeye gaze. No symptom of anxiety, stage fright. So depressed he doesn't care what we think. But he cares enough to come to class and talk. Good sign. "And you don't really change that much," Mick continues. "You do different things, and try different things, but you always come back to the way you are."

Fatima says softly: "An innate self." She's so wise, I wish she'd speak up more.

Mick: "An innate self, yeah. So, for example, when you get drunk..." Giggles, whispers, from direction of Bad Lacrosse Guy.

"Hey, quiet back there!" I say. "Can everyone hear what Mick is saying? Okay, he is trying to say that we all have a core self that never really changes. Is that a fair paraphrase?"

Mick: "Yeah. If you're drunk, obviously on one level your brain is not working properly. But at the same time, part of you still sees things clearly, the same way as when you're sober."

Yeah, I've been there. Getting drunk when you're depressed is like pouring water on a stone. Tell Mick that? No, getting too heavy. Lighten things up, smile. "Maybe you see things clearly when you're drunk, but that has not been my experience." Mick looks steadily at me as others giggle. Shit, he thinks I'm making fun of him.

Fatima: "I agree with Mick that you have one self that is true to your values and how you actually feel. And then you have the persona that is more acceptable to everyone else, the persona that you show to other people, what you think everyone else wants to see. So you're just altering yourself to please everyone else. But deep down inside, that's how you actually are. That's where your real thoughts are."

Look into her lovely intelligent brown eyes, wonder what her real thoughts are right now. "Yes, good point, Fatima. And actually, you have a lot of public selves, right? You have one self for a situation like this, in a classroom, versus when you're with your family or boyfriend or girlfriend. So all of us have these different personas, which to a certain extent are acting. Playing a role."

Tell them about *anatta*? Sure, why not. "Some Buddhists have a radical hypothesis about the self, which is called *anatta*. They say when you meditate, you should look at all your thoughts and ask, Where am I in these thoughts? And you realize, as each thought comes and goes, That's not me, that's just a passing thought. If you keep doing this, you discover that underlying all your thoughts, perceptions, memories, emotions—everything that makes you what you are—there is this emptiness, or pure consciousness, that's not unique to you. Your own personal, unique, individual self doesn't exist. There is only one Big Self, that we all share." Look at them looking at me, wondering what the hell I'm talking about. Class almost over, but still time for James on mysticism.

"James was also fascinated by these experiences that many people throughout history have had, where they feel like they're seeing Reality with a capital R. They leave Plato's cave and see the Sun. These are called mystical experiences. James was desperate to have one. He even took drugs that could supposedly trigger mystical experiences. Peyote, for example, which just made him sick. He also sniffed nitrous oxide, laughing gas. When he was high, he wrote down his insights. Once he wrote, Good and evil reconciled in a laugh, which is pretty profound. But most of what he wrote was gibberish, which isn't surprising. James himself said that mystical insights are ineffable, which means they can't be put into words. Except maybe, Wow! or Holy Cow!" Waggle hands and bug eyes out for comic effect.

Mick, unsmiling: "Do you believe in God?"

Damn. Should I give him a serious or jokey answer? "It depends on what kind of day I'm having," I say. Smile at him. "Usually I call myself an agnostic. Does everyone know what agnostic means? It means I'm completely mystified by the world." Glance again at my watch.

"Any questions?" Students already zipping open backpacks, stuffing books inside. Used to think this was rude, now it's no big deal. "If you have one takeaway from James"—loudly so they can hear me over the noise they're making—"I hope it's that you think about your own thinking a little more." Everyone poised to leave. Watching me. "All right! Thanks for a great discussion. We will talk about Freud on Thursday. Have something to say about the differences between Freud and James. Okay?"

Students file out chitchatting or staring dully at nothing. Turn off recorder, go to whiteboard. Erase WILLIAM JAMES PSYCHOLOGY DESCARTES SOLIPSISM ESP QUANTUM NONLOCALITY ANATTA MYSTICISM.

Lots of digressions. I used to worry about digressing in class, felt self-indulgent, unprofessional. Then I thought, I'm the Fucking Professor! What professors say is important by *definition*. And who's to say what's a digression, what's important? Digressions are like spandrels, start out as pointless side effects of important things, things with a purpose, but end up becoming important themselves. Yeah, that's good, should riff on that next class.

Exit Althofer onto street thronged with chattering cheerful students. A mini-surge of optimism wells up in me. From upbeat thoughts about young people? Maybe, but mostly from relief, post-class endorphins kicking in. No more teaching today, I'm free! Until tomorrow.

I shouldn't see teaching that way, I should cherish the chance to shape young minds. Emily scolds me for being compulsive about finishing things, calls me a completionist, someone who sees life as a series of chores, items to tick off my To Do list. I finish a class or blog post and exult, Done! Even good things.

Sexual intercourse, Done! She says when I die, my last thought will be, Done! Bugs me when she says that because she might be right.

Enter Humanities again, ascend stairs again. Up down, up down, like Sisyphus, getting nowhere. But if it's fun, it's not pointless. Even if it's not fun, it's worth Paying Attention to. Paying Attention makes it matter. Chop wood, teach freshman Humanities class.

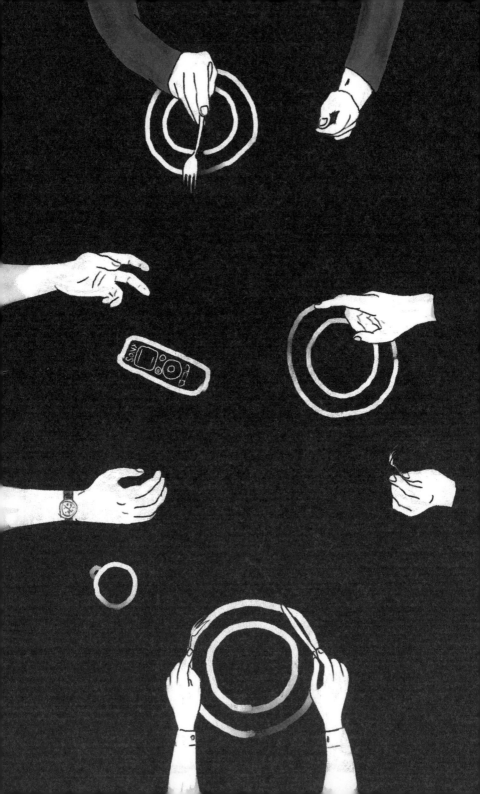

Chapter 4

Eating Lunch
at the Faculty Club

Re-enter office, 11:32, lunch with Jim at noon. What should I do until then? Take notes on the class while it's still fresh, stuff not on the recorder, what I was thinking while teaching. There was something I was supposed to remember, write down. What was it? Something about an animal. Bat? Gorilla? If I can't remember, it doesn't matter.

Should write a column about my long-running debate with Jim. Honest-to-God postmodernist, studied with Kuhn in the '70s, says science can't prove or disprove things, we can't know anything with certainty, there's no absolute permanent truth. I say, What about the Earth being round and not flat? The Earth isn't round, Jim replies, it's an oblate spheroid! So it's an oblate spheroid! I say. *That's* the truth! Since then, whenever Jim starts with his postmodern nonsense, I yell, Oblate spheroid! Oblate spheroid!

Emily mocks my obsession with philosophy and scientific topics distant from real, everyday concerns. Calls it the Big Bang and All That Stuff. She wants me to write about real problems. Like why do some women hardly ever have orgasms? What causes premenstrual syndrome? Menopause? Why would Natural Selection design women so badly, hmm? She says, If men got PMS and hot flashes, you *know* we'd have better theories and treatments. I reply, I'm a man, and I have often wished that scientists would cure PMS.

Emily says menopause is no big deal for some women, but others have hot flashes so intense and sweaty they need waterproof sheets. Male scientists assume women are all the same, but they're all different. She once took a class on female sexuality, and the teacher passed around a book filled with photos of vaginas. Some are just neat little slits, others are big droopy multilayered complicated things. Hard to believe it's all the same organ from the same species.

I loved that. Mention diversity of vaginas next time I tell students about dangers of reductionism? No, probably not. Maybe write a column: Vaginas and the Limits of Reductionism. Wait: Vaginas and the Limits of Science. Yeah, more dramatic. Illustrate with photo montage of vaginas, push boundaries of science journalism. Run by editors, convince them column will be tasteful, excellent traffic-booster.

"Toole! Lunch?" Jim at the door, eyebrows raised, head cocked, hair looking fantastic.

"Professor McDorn! I was just thinking about vaginas."

"You mean sometimes you don't?"

Jim looks like a college professor should look. Splendid, curly white hair and beard, Old Testament, like Moses. Except Jim's not super-serious like Moses, more like Moses's wise-ass kid brother, rolls his eyes and cracks smutty jokes when Moses preaches. Hey, what if my neighbor's wife covets *my* ass, Moses? Huh? Can I go for it? Will God smite me? Jim likes to joke about sex, gay and straight. Sometimes he blows air kisses at me to make me blush, to his delight. Wears a black academic gown when teaching. I love seeing him rush to class, gown billowing behind him. No gown now, he's wearing an orange V-neck sweater over a white Oxford shirt.

"Ahh!" I push my palms toward him and avert my eyes as he approaches. "Your sweater is blinding me!"

"It's a present from my wife, asshole. You free for lunch or what?"

"Of course. You going right now?"

"Yup. Gonna see if Dave wants to join us."

"Great. Faculty Club?"

"Yeah."

"Okay, let's go."

Language can be an amazingly effective tool, enabling unambiguous social transactions. Good for postmodern Humanities types like Jim to keep in mind when going on about the ineffability of reality, limits of language, blah blah blah.

Slip digital recorder in pocket, walk with Jim down the hall to Math Department. Jim pokes his head in an office. "Hilbert! Wanna come to lunch with me and Toole?"

"Sure!"

Dave emerges from the office. Jacket, tie, silver crew cut. Nice guy, almost eccentric in his lack of eccentricity, especially for a mathematician. They tend toward weirdness, like Conway, inventor of Game of Life, a cellular automaton that generates endless novelty from simple rules. Like quasicrystals, Penrose tiles. Conway looked like a homeless nut when I interviewed him at Princeton, stringy hair down to his waist, pants unbelted, slumping, ass crack exposed. Mathematicians the most rational of all creatures and the nuttiest. Except for Dave.

"I like hanging out with you fuzzy-minded Humanities people," Dave says.

"Don't mathematicians practice fuzzy logic?" I ask.

"Yeah, that used to be a thing," Dave says. "But even our fuzziest logic isn't as fuzzy as Humanities logic." Coming from Dave, the joke is gentle, affectionate, not mean.

"Hilbert," Jim says, "I didn't think you were the type of guy to kick the Humanities when they're down."

Dave, smiling: "That reminds me of something a philosopher at MIT once told me. He complained to a physicist about how philosophy gets no respect, and the physicist said, We count, you don't."

"Ouch!" Jim says.

Strolling uphill toward the administration high-rise, we converge with François, and Jim asks him to join us. François is a physicist-engineer, gourmet, oenophile, French, accent thick as Hollandaise. François is a Know-It-All, and he brings out the Know-It-All in me. We butt heads over the neural code, unified theory of physics, roots of war. He spouts opinions at me, I spout back. What happens when two Know-It-Alls butt heads? For bystanders, extreme boredom.

Once I was pontificating about the evils of biological determinism, and François counter-pontificated that professors shouldn't pass judgment on ideas, they should help students reach their own judgments. Determinism, Social Darwinism, Eugenics aren't intrinsically bad, they're just abused by humans. François summarized grandly, There are no Bad Ideas. I said, *That* is a Bad Idea. My reward was a scowl from François and a *Touche!* from Jim.

Take the elevator to the Faculty Club, 4th floor of administration building, overlooking the Hudson and Manhattan. Load trays with food, find empty table. As my friends take their seats, I explain my Pay Attention Project to them and ask if I can record our lunch conversation. They say I must be desperate for material, my writing career is obviously going off the rails, they'd demand a cut of the royalties but obviously there won't be any. And so on. I respond that I wanted to record a lunch with younger, smarter, prettier professors, like Lisa, Jessica and Dawn, but they were too busy, unlike you Cranky Old Farts.

Jim, Dave and François watch with amusement as I take my recorder out, turn it on, place it on the table, red light glowing.

"So Jim," I say, "I need advice from you. Tomorrow in my history of science class I'm going to talk about Lavoisier, the invention of modern chemistry, blah blah blah. And here's what I need to know: Is it phlo-*gis*-ton, or *phlo*-gis-ton? I can never remember."

Jim eyes me suspiciously. "Phlo-*gis*-ton."

François, expert on all things European and scientific, nods sagely. "Yes, that's right."

I can't stop myself from baiting Jim my postmodern friend, just as I bait Christians, Buddhists, Evo Psychos, Freudians, Singularitarians. True Believers in Bad Ideas. Jim is a True Unbeliever, almost as bad as a True Believer. I say, "I love telling my students about the triumph of modern science over phlo-*gis*-ton, alchemy and all that bullshit primitive pseudoscience."

Jim, his mouth full of greens, shakes his head vigorously and emits muffled protests. "Mmmm! Mmm!"

I swallow a bite of stir-fried noodles. "Don't worry. I give them your postmodern view, and then I tell them why it's wrong. Lavoisier discovered oxygen and figured out its role in combustion and showed that the phlo-*gis*-ton theory of combustion was wrong."

Jim, after gulping his food down: "Let me just interject. You can say my position is bullshit and your realist position is whatever it is. But to go back and call alchemy and phlogiston pseudoscience is, I think, a mistake."

Jim loves reminding us that Newton filled notebooks with descriptions of wacky alchemy experiments and religious ravings. The Hero of the Enlightenment was a Crank.

Me: "So I guess I shouldn't have told them that geocentric astronomy was pseudoscience."

Jim: "Yeah! Alchemy and geocentric astronomy are models for science!"

I look at Jim. "Okay, I think we should settle this once and for all. This thing you have about scientific"—I claw the air with curly forefingers—"'truth.'"

Jim, with calm warrior confidence: "Bring it on."

Dave: "Uh oh."

Me, ignoring Dave: "Jim, obviously you are a very well-educated person."

Jim, with extra sarcasm: "Thank you."

Me: "You're a scholar! Professor! Esteemed historian of science! And yet you don't really believe science is capable of producing truth."

François, wearily: "Oh, God. Not this again."

I glance at François, weighing the pros and cons of an alliance. "François, I forget what your position is on scientific truth."

François, with oodles of Hollandaise: "My position is very nuanced."

Jim chuckles. "Mine is not. And I can give it to you quite easily. Science is *stories* we tell about nature. And some stories are better than other stories. And you can compare stories to each other on all kinds of grounds, but you have no access to"—he pauses for dramatic effect—"The Truth. Or any mode of knowing outside of your own storytelling capabilities, which include rationality, experiment, explanatory scope and the whole thing. I would love to have some means of making knowledge about the world that would allow us to say, This is really it. There really are goddamn electrons." He thumps the table.

Me: "What about elements! You can't be sure elements are real? The discovery of elements is just another story?"

Jim, stabbing a cherry tomato with his fork: "Yeah, it's a story, because what do you mean by an element? In 1880 you mean one thing by an element. Post-Einstein you mean something else by an element. And post-Higgs boson you have another view. There's no one thing, element. It's a set of sentences that we make and say, That's an element."

Me: "So the implication of your view is that you can never say that science converges on the truth. If we keep practicing science, we will keep generating new theories, new *stories* that we tell about nature, forever."

Jim: "I would say so."

François, thrusting his bottom lip forward, says to Jim: "You are full of bullshit."

I cheer, Dave and Jim guffaw.

"Postmodernism is bullshit," François continues, pleased with our reactions. He lifts his glass of iced tea. "I mean, I firmly believe this glass of iced tea is cold now, and after a while it will get warm. And that demonstrates the truth of the Second Law of Thermodynamics."

Jim: "Okay, this is a very good example. So the idea that this glass isn't cold or that there is no evolution or something, those are stories we want to reject, just like we reject geocentrism. But still, what we mean by the story is not a fixed thing. What we mean by evolution, what we mean by the Second Law of Thermodynamics, keeps changing."

François, squinting skeptically at Jim: "In science we rarely go backward. We go forward and explain a much larger set of data. And it becomes harder and harder to contradict those. So I don't think we will ever go back and say, We have to give up the theory of the elements."

Jim, jabbing the air with his fork, talking fast: "But the question is, what are we comparing our theories about nature *to*? We can always say the claims we're making now are superior to previous claims based on this and that and the other thing. If you want to call that truth, I don't have a problem with it. But *he*"—pointing his fork at me—"thinks truth is this absolute, objective thing outside of ourselves that we can know. And he uses things like elements as examples. But these are moving targets! The truth is not the same thing at any moment of time!"

François: "That's where I disagree. I think at some point there is universal agreement, like on the existence of elements."

I nod vigorously. François is coming through. I want to clap him on the back.

Jim: "Yeah, there is universal agreement. But what do we mean by that? For most of the 19th century, elements didn't have any parts. Now, suddenly, they got parts! They got atoms and protons and neutrons and electrons. Whoa! And then *those* things have parts, and *those* things have parts."

François, serenely: "That doesn't bother me." François is a very smart, sensible guy, more than I've given him credit for.

Jim, agitated: "It doesn't bother me either! But you can't say there is one thing: an element. It's a set of sentences that we have at this point in time, and we say, These are elements. And I agree! It's a hell of a story!"

Me: "Was it Kuhn who made you this way? Did he brainwash you when you were his grad student?"

Jim: "Absolutely."

Me: "Seriously? You didn't believe all this postmodern shit before..."

Jim: "No! I was just a kid before I met Kuhn! And I grew up with this '50s mentality about science: Science is true, it eliminates superstition, it's got this great scientific method, and it churns out true facts about nature."

Me: "You used to be a naïve realist like me."

Jim: "Of course! By the way, Kuhn was a realist. He actually believed there is a real world out here. It's just unknowable. But he wasn't naïve, like you are. He was a genius."

Me: "Kuhn was so weird. When I interviewed him, and he was explaining his philosophy to me, I felt like he took too much LSD or something."

Jim snorts: "You can *never* take too much LSD." Jim, Columbia Class of '68, is still a hippy radical at heart, bless him.

Me: "Kuhn seemed to think all this reality we live in is… *Maya.* You know, illusion. And we can never know the truth behind all these transitory forms. Real mystical hippy shit. I mean, part of me, the old flaky acidhead part, agrees with Kuhn about that. But the rational science journalist in me says, There *is* such a thing as truth, and we can discover it through these various means."

Jim, with a sly smile: "Toole, what's going on in your psyche that makes you have this need to *know?*"

Dave, quietly chewing noodles, watches us with amused detachment. I wonder if Dave can help me. He's a mathematician, a believer in logic, deduction, proof. Maybe math is getting postmodern, Gödelian, and hard for ordinary mortals to understand, but 1 + 1 still equals 2, the Pythagorean Theorem is still true. "Dave," I ask, "most mathematicians believe in Truth with a capital T, right?"

Dave, in his mild, unflappable way: "Well, it depends what you mean. Most mathematicians would say they believe in proof from axioms. You start with these assumptions, and then you prove something, and that means something. But as to whether the axioms hold or not…" He shrugs.

Me, heart sinking: "Okay, but you don't agree with this idea that all our knowledge is constructed, do you? Aren't most mathematicians Platonists? Who believe mathematical truth exists out there? Apart from us?"

Dave: "Well, most of us do believe in some not very well articulated way that there are absolute mathematical objects, which we discover." He pauses, tipping his head quizzically. "And you do have to wonder why math seems so unreasonably effective in describing the physical world."

François pounces: "It's just luck."

Dave, amused: "Just luck?"

François: "Yeah. We develop all these mathematical tools, like catastrophe theory, and bifurcation theory." He sticks out his lower lip and shrugs. "Some tools turn out to have practical value, they are useful. But it's purely coincidental."

Dave, putting his hand on my shoulder and smirking: "And some *Tooles* turn out to be useless."

Dave is too nice to hurt my feelings. "Ha ha," I say, and go back on the offensive. "But most physicists don't just think of math as tools that are invented. They think there is mathematical order out there in the world, and we are discovering it."

Jim: "I would say that the *tools* we're using to explore the natural world give us what it is that we discover."

Me, sneering: "Yeah, I can guess the rest. We confuse our tools and maps and theories with reality, right?"

Jim: "Yeah! And there's no other way to know the reality. You can't call God and say, What's the *real* reality?"

Something moving outside the window catches my eye. An ocean liner, like a skyscraper on its side, cruises up the Hudson. So huge! Like the Enormous Theorem, its proof more than 15,000 pages long, made of sub-proofs by over a hundred different mathematicians, as hideously complex as the blueprint for an ocean liner, or jumbo jet. No one really grokked the Enormous Theorem except Gorenstein, the general contractor, who died before the proof was finished. Bring up the Enormous Theorem? No, too much of a digression. I turn to Dave again and ask, "Is it because of Gödel that you can't be sure about mathematical truth?" Gödel became paranoid, so scared of being poisoned that he starved himself to death. Talk about a flaw in your logic.

Dave: "No, it's not that you can't be sure about mathematical proof. Gödel just showed that, whatever your axioms are, except for very simple cases, there will be statements in those axioms that you can't prove are either true or false."

Me: "So do mathematicians actually worry about that?"

Dave: "No, we don't. Maybe we should worry more about the logical foundations of mathematics, because basically there aren't any." He smiles, shrugs. "And yet we don't really worry about it."

Me: "Because math works! Math gave us the H-bomb! Math put Whitey on the Moon!"

Jim, smiling indulgently: "Math leads to useful results."

Dave: "Yeah." Pause. "Tenure, for example."

Jim: "Oh ho ho!"

Me, losing hope that Dave will help me crush Jim: "Dave, what about scientific truth? Do you agree with me that science can uncover genuine truth, or is it all storytelling, like Jim says?"

Dave: "Well, you do seem to have a succession of more and more accurate theories. But it could be that there is no limit to this series of theories. Then I guess you'd have to say that there is no truth out there waiting for us to find it, like Jim says."

Jim, food in mouth, triumphantly: "Mmm hmm!"

Me, after a theatrical sigh: "So here's the problem I have with Jim's theory."

Jim: "It's not a theory."

Me: "Yeah, you're right. Theory gives you too much credit. I mean your... view. Your attitude. Your"—sneering—"*opinion*."

Jim: "Ha ha ha."

Me: "There are areas of science where progress is very rapid. Even postmodernists have to grant that physicists in the first half of the 20th century were doing experiments that produced completely novel and unexpected results, leading to rapid advances in theory, which then led to more predictions and confirmations and so on."

Jim: "Like the Bomb."

Me: "Exactly! Talk about a confirmation of your paradigm. Then you have fields like psychology. There are all these books now on neuroscience and psychology that say Buddhism might be the best solution for mental problems like depression and anxiety. Buddhism! Invented thousands of years ago!"

Jim: "What's wrong with that?"

Me: "That would be like physicists at the Large Hadron Collider saying, You know what? We just discovered that the ancient Greeks were right after all. There are only four elements: Earth, Wind, Fire and... Shit, what's the fourth element? I always forget."

Jim: "Water. And it's Air, not Wind. You're thinking of the old rock group. Okay, let me give you the Kuhnian answer to what you just said. In psychology there's no paradigm or frame of reference that all researchers are going to agree upon, which gives you the problems you are going to research and the techniques you are going to use. It's possible that you will have paradigmatic research at some point, just not yet."

François: "I have no doubt that 50 years from now we will have a much more deterministic view of what the brain does."

Jim: "Okay. But whether scientists agree on a paradigm or not is no test of the success or truth value of any of these sets of claims. We can't use these different degrees of maturity of these different inquiries as the basis to say something about their truth value."

Me: "You've already granted there are ways of judging the relative merits of different theories. If it's possible to make those sorts of comparisons, then you've got some kind of transcendent standard of truth."

Jim: "No, you don't. You have a comparison of apples and oranges."

Me: "What?! No, come on. Surely you're not saying that."

Jim: "Of course I am! That's exactly what I'm saying. Some stories are better than others, and you determine that..."

Me: "Yeah, but apples and oranges means it's just a matter of taste."

Jim: "No, that I don't mean. There are criteria that can help you make judgments. Explanatory scope, applicability, evidence of one sort or another. It would be those things that would allow you to say theory A is better than theory B. But you can't say theory A is true and theory B is false. They're different. Apples and oranges."

Me, staring at him: "Are most historians of science…"

Dave: "Are they as crazy as you are?" Everyone laughs, Jim hardest.

Me: "What's infuriating to me is that a lot of super-smart people think if you're super-smart you should have this subtle postmodern view of truth."

Jim, gleeful: "Oooooh! So that explains it! Now we're getting to the bottom of this! Your psychological need!"

I'm getting too serious, shrill, self-righteous, like when I lecture Emily on homeopathy, but I can't stop. "It's not a psychological need, Jim. It's actually a political and moral issue. Let's say we're talking about projections of Global Warming and whether they are strong enough to merit various aggressive countermeasures. Or the challenges of creationists to evolution. I think—I *know*—that postmodernism undermines the ability of scientists to prevail in these debates."

Dave, derisively: "Yeah, because all those people in the Bible Belt are reading Kuhn or Bruno Latour."

Me: "It happens!"

Dave, eyebrows raised: "It does?"

François: "The people in the Bible Belt are postmodern?"

Me: "Listen, you probably wouldn't think fundamentalists would read someone like Steve Gould, but they did. When he started critiquing conventional Darwinian dogma back in the '80s, the creationists loved it, they all quoted him. Gould was appalled. He had to scale back his rhetoric."

Jim, serious now, seeing how serious I am: "This seems like a phony argument. So scholars have developed these very sophisticated views of what knowledge is, how we create knowledge, how we express it, what is communication, what is language, what are words."

François, amused: "Is there a postmodern exegesis of the Bible?" He pronounces *exegesis* as if it were a delicious hors d'oeuvre, like escargot.

Jim, sternly: "Let me just finish my thought. I don't see how all this undermines a liberal, progressive, morally sensitive set of arguments about the issues that we face today. Postmodernism, all this stuff we've been talking about, is completely irrelevant to politics."

François: "It's really just liberal versus conservative. That has nothing to do with truth."

Me: "You're wrong. If you're the kind of postmodernist who says all truth claims serve the purposes of the group that's making them, that undercuts the whole point of arguing on the basis of facts and evidence. My job as a science journalist is to say, I think this is bullshit, or, This makes sense to me, and here's the evidence. And if some professor, some smart person like you..."

Jim, laughing: "Smart *ass!*"

Me: "You're saying, Well, this is a good *story*. Some people like this *story*, but, hey! This is a good *story* too! That's a huge problem."

Jim. "Okay, let's even grant that. But it doesn't seem to me that you want to then become a naïve realist, and think there are no issues here about how knowledge is constructed."

Me: "I realize there are certain arbitrary, cultural, constructed aspects of our knowledge. But when it comes to elements and electrons and atoms, after a while we can forget all that Kuhnian postmodern stuff, because the evidence is so overwhelming. When we look at psychology or behavioral genetics, and scientists are saying there's a Warrior Gene, which explains why certain ethnic groups are more violent than others, *then* you need to think about how racism and politics and all those things affect science."

Jim: "You can enlist postmodernism in your campaign! If you think there is a gene for criminality, or homosexuality, you could say, Well, look at the social construction of knowledge. Look at the egregious claims made by really qualified scientists about intelligence or whatnot."

Me: "I do that all the time. But that skeptical, postmodern treatment is justified if you're talking about behavioral genetics, because it has produced one outrageously crappy claim after another, none of which has held up. Like the schizophrenia gene, and the gay gene, and the high-IQ gene. But that's not true of fields like nuclear physics, where you get real progress."

Jim: "Well, I wouldn't use the word *progress*. There are some things that we know more reliably, that are less impacted by social and political factors in the community constructing this knowledge. You can see that in physics. But Newton's world, his physics, his science, is nothing like the world of modern physics. Space and time are different. Mass is convertible to energy for Einstein, not for Newton. The whole schmagoogle. It's a different world!"

Me: "*Schmagoogle?*"

Jim: "*Schmagoogle.* A good Yiddish term. Look, some things are more, uh, foundational than others. Thermodynamics is foundational. It's going to take a lot to overturn thermodynamics. Biological evolution is another one. So you're going to be hard pressed to have a worldview that doesn't have some version of those."

Dave: "So you might call them almost true."

Jim: "Yeah! Almost true, man."

Me: "So you grant that some paradigms are so effective that you might as well call them true."

Jim, laughing: "I like that! You might as well call it truth! Fine!"

François: "Truth with a small t!"

I'm dissatisfied with this quasi-concession, quasi-resolution. I want total victory, unconditional surrender. But I need to let it go. Persistence after a certain point becomes inappropriate, a category error, like throwing your racket at your tennis opponent. I have consumed my stir-fried noodles and drunk my iced tea. I lift my glass, tip an ice cube into my mouth, crush it between my teeth.

Dave stands, holding his tray, Jim, François and I do likewise. Surveying my half-eaten cheesecake, I feel a twinge of guilt. What would Singer think? He would calculate how much the calories in this uneaten cake could extend a starving child's life. Dave nods at my digital recorder, red light still glowing. "Don't forget your thingie."

Turn recorder off, slip in pocket. "You guys were great. I'm going to put this lunch in a book and make you famous. Of course I'm going to edit it to make myself sound smarter and all of you sound dumber. Except Jim. I can't make him sound dumber." Grab Jim by the shoulder and shake him, growling, "Rrrrrrrrrrr!" He spins, mock punches me, laughs as I mutter through clenched teeth, "Oblate spheroid, oblate spheroid."

Chapter 5

Riding the Ferry to Manhattan

Stroll with Jim, Dave and François from the Howe Center, swapping gossip about school officials. François peels off toward Engineering. "See you guys." "Okay, have a good one." "Bye." "Au revoir." Dave, Jim and I enter Humanities and repeat the farewell ritual. "So long." "Later man." "Yeah later."

Watch passively as robot body clumps up stairs, sticks key in office door, slumps into chair. Repeat, repeat. Tired, time for a boost. Wake Up! coffee candy, Mocha Mint. Yum. Brood over lunch conversation. Jim's a good guy, reasonable, wise, a wise wiseass. Baffling when someone I like and respect disagrees with me on something important, like whether science gives us Truth. Pretty fucking important. If reason is reason, shouldn't it take us all to the same place? Like that kid said in class, Dragon Tattoo. 1 + 1 = 2, Earth is an oblate spheroid, science discovers truth.

Jim thinks I'm the one who's irrational. He's a hardcore atheist, loves teasing me about my Catholic roots. I once confessed how I lost my faith. Six or seven, in a snowball fight with older kids, hiding behind a bush, I *knew* God would protect me. Stood up, filled with faith, and an ice ball smacked me in the eye. I cried, more in disappointment than pain. Jim found the story hilarious, said it explained everything. Toole, you replaced Faith in God with Faith in Science!

That's bullshit, I'm skeptical of science, just not as skeptical as Jim. Jim's too skeptical, Emily's not skeptical enough. She believes in homeopathy! Astrology! Tarot! I don't mock her, out of respect, love, desire for continued sexual relations. Well, sometimes I mock her, but not often. When she gives me a Tarot reading, part of me cares what she says, the superstitious, irrational part. I wish I could ask her to pull cards, give me advice on whether to ask The Question tonight, but The Question is about her.

My reason isn't exactly infallible, certainly not when it comes to my love life. Reason is a smug Know-It-All in my brain telling my emotional self what to do. Toward the end of my marriage, Know-It-All informs me: I have rationally assessed the situation, and I know what's happening, what's best for you, Tricia and the kids. Tricia is going through premenopausal craziness, a biochemical hormonal phase, but she still loves you, deep down. Be patient, show her how much you love her, cherish her. She'll come around, things will be okay.

Next month Know-It-All reassesses: Tricia is a crazy bitch, she never loved you, she's poison, you need to get away from her, move to Hoboken, get an apartment near school, find a woman who loves you, or at least likes you, enough to have sex with you. Better yet lots of women. Yeah, why not! Have some fun before you're too old. So I find an apartment in Hoboken, get ready to put a deposit down. Then Know-It-All re-reassesses and yells, like it's my fault: What the fuck are you doing? If you move to Hoboken, you'll never see Neal and Claire, fool! What kind of father are you! Everything Tricia said about you is true!

New plan: Move to Cold Spring apartment, walking distance from high school, so kids can come over any time, walking distance from the train station, makes commute to Hoboken easier. That worked fine, especially after I quit drinking, went on Match.com, met Emily. Smart, loving lady with good job, nice apartment.

After a year start having doubts, looking at other women, fantasizing. Know-It-All re-emerges and issues new assessment: If you really loved Emily, you wouldn't think about other women. You hooked up with her too fast, when you were still rebounding from Tricia. You should have dated more women, for Emily's sake, not just yours. She deserves a guy who loves her so much he never *thinks* about other women.

Should have ignored fucking Know-It-All. But one morning at Emily's place I suggest, joking, not joking, that we try a little experiment, dating other people. Emily shocked, thought things were great, doesn't want to be with me if I want to be with other women. Starts crying, telling me to leave. Her reaction dismays me. I wasn't even entirely serious! But Know-It-All assures me this is for the best. I should seek a new mate, one so amazing I never think about other women. And maybe someone less into pseudoscience, although that's not a deal-breaker, sexual compatibility is more important. And Emily should find a guy who really loves her. This is for her as much as for me.

I go back on Match.com, meet a few ladies, but I miss Emily, can't stop thinking about her, fantasizing about her. Know-It-All has the gall to say, You fucking idiot! You broke up with the smartest, most loving woman you've ever known! After nights of feverish half-sleep, I call Emily, tell her how much I miss her, beg her to take me back. Plead temporary insanity, a loopy program hijacked my brain, but I have fully recovered. I promise I will never break up with her again, never stop loving her.

She has moved on, dating other guys, really likes one, a psychiatrist at Columbia. I Google him, he sounds pretty cool, researches links between inflammation and depression. But I make fun of his name, looks, research. I call him Dr. Quack. Emily protests, He's not a quack! He's at Columbia! But I can tell she likes me fighting for her. She lets me woo her, take her out on a few dates, finally takes me back. Months later she mentions the psychiatrist's inflammation theory, can't remember his name, calls him Dr. Quack. Yes! My victory is complete.

Our breakup still feels like something that happened to me, not really my choice, my responsibility. Emily rolls her eyes when I say *our breakup*, as though it was mutual. She insists on *The Dumping*. My behavior confirmed what she suspected: I'm not a very loving guy, deep down I'm cold. She has a name for this too: The Coldness. She loves me in spite of my flaws, but not as much as before The Dumping. My coldness made her a little cold too.

When she reminds me of The Dumping, and The Coldness, part of me thinks: I have to earn back her trust and love, by showing her how much I love her. Another part thinks: Our breakup happened years ago, she should have forgiven me by now, she's being a bitch, maybe we shouldn't be together. But I promised her.

Ding! New email. From Emily! Her reply to my reply to the chihuahua-elephant video she sent. *XOXOXO see you tonite Monkey Man!* She always adds kisses and hugs, they don't mean anything. But still, she's out there now, thinking of me, I'm thinking of her. Are we psychically connected via spooky quantum force field? No. Maybe. Who the fuck knows. Tonight, I will definitely ask The Question. I choose to ask, of my own Free Will, after careful rational assessment, weighing of pros and cons.

3:45. Stay in office longer or head to ferry? I'm catching the ferry sooner or later, so not a real choice, only a matter of timing, like Libet's stupid experiment, favorite of Free Will Deniers. Deciding when to push a button in a lab isn't a real choice, it's only a matter of timing! Not like deciding whether to study journalism or geology, write about Free Will or antidepressants, ask a woman to marry you. Those are real, consequential choices, based on conscious, rational analysis, weighing of pros and cons. Right?

Yeah, but maybe those choices are foregone conclusions too. Maybe we're all like that poor epileptic woman Wegner wrote about. Researchers cut a hole in her skull, stick electrodes in her brain, zap it, make her arm fly up. When researchers ask why she lifted her arm, she says, I was waving to that cute doctor! They stimulate another spot that makes her giggle, and she says, You look so funny! Intention Invention, Wegner calls it. Telling stories to ourselves, why we do what we do. We all do it, Intention Invention. Tell ourselves tales, confabulate.

Trivers says deceit is adaptive, good for seducing women, crushing rivals, propagating genes. Self-deceit is adaptive too, because we lie more persuasively, with fewer tells, if we believe our own bullshit. I worried about inviting Trivers to school.

Bipolar, hot-tempered, all the rest. But he was cool, a hipster in sunglasses, leather jacket, knitted Rasta cap, prowling around the auditorium with a wolfish lope, riffing in his Tom Waits growl, calling us Man and Brother. Students loved him. He used to lie a lot to girlfriends, wives, friends, colleagues, and to himself, but studying deception and self-deception made him more self-aware, more honest with others and himself.

That's what he told me, but he's fooling himself, he can't stop lying, he's doomed to fail, we all are. Earnest, goody-goody, bullshit-detecting Superego is always one step behind the sneaky, manic, bullshitting Id. No, it's worse than that, it's a Cold War in our heads, *Spy Vs. Spy*. Our minds swarm with agents and double agents with secret agendas, spreading disinformation. There is no omniscient, central self that really knows what's going on. Knowing you are an unreliable narrator doesn't make you reliable.

The only way to stop self-deception is to live like a hermit, throw yourself into solitary confinement, ruthlessly interrogate yourself. No, even then you'll still confabulate. Buddha, the ultimate Know-It-All, said, I've solved the problem of life, people! I can end your suffering! Yeah, right, Buddha, tell us another one. What about your wife and kids, huh? What about how *they* suffered when you split to seek enlightenment?

Studying the mind should give you more self-knowledge and self-control, make you happier and nicer, but where's the evidence? James was haunted by fear and melancholy throughout his life. Freud was an egomaniac, liar and bully. Jung had a psychotic breakdown, had to be nursed back to health by his wife and mistress. At least Trivers has bipolar disorder as an excuse.

Maybe introspection, trying to know ourselves, just makes our self-deceptions more elaborate. We use reason, arguing skills, to fool ourselves. I once lectured Neal and Claire on the perils of being a drunk or druggie, and I said the worst thing is the lying. You start lying to others and eventually to yourself, and you don't know the difference anymore between lies and truth. Then you're lost, your whole life is lies, you end up lonely and miserable, a stranger even to yourself. Standard fatherly wisdom, but as I'm talking I'm thinking, This is bullshit.

Maybe the key to happiness is to stop doubting yourself, embrace your delusions. Because the lies we tell ourselves can come true. If you really believe you're the world's greatest lover, warrior, scientist, prophet, guru, businessman, your belief might become self-fulfilling. You can become Casanova, Napoleon, Freud, Mohammed, Buddha. All you have to do is persuade others to believe you too. Lying leads to unhappiness is just another lie of parents and professors, like the unexamined life is not worth living.

Ding. Email from Melanie, my bipolar friend, a poet and science writer. Hope she's taking my advice, writing about her illness, turning pain into material. My solution for everything.

Melanie: *Don't worry, I have no plans to get ECT right now. I'm just interested in it.* [Phew.] *And I'm still managing to do a little writing in my journal. But I have to admit there's something I worry about.* [Uh oh.] *Suppose I ever somehow did write a book on my illness and get it published (and that is a major suppose). I know your public persona, and I can imagine you first saying something nice but then tearing it apart (on some subtopic like pharmaceuticals or therapy or whatever). All in the interest of good intellectual debate. I've never had thick skin, and this topic is where the intellect meets the emotional road. Just saying...*

Really? She thinks I'd do that? I'm only an asshole to assholes!
To people who deserve it! Who can take it! Like Gell-Mann!
Edelman!

I reply: *Melanie, I promise I will never say anything that might upset
you. Of course others might. The critical reception to any writer's
work can be brutal, even when well-intentioned. Some of the cruelest
comments I've gotten have been thoughtless remarks by friends. You
also have to deal with envy if your book does well. And if you're
writing about something so agonizingly personal as mental illness,
you're especially vulnerable. Ultimately, my advice is always to write
for its own sake, not for money, fame, impact, etc. If you find the
writing itself meaningful, and fulfilling, go for it. If you don't, then
let it go. This must sound so glib! But that's the best advice I can
offer. Eamon.*

Edelman was definitely an asshole, monster ego, won Nobel
for some immune thing and then thought he could solve
consciousness. Weird guy, kept cracking unfunny jokes,
comparing himself to God. Arrogance blinded him, preventing
him from seeing weaknesses of his consciousness theory, just
a neural network wrapped in clunky new jargon. Years after I
dissed him, we ended up together at a meeting on the limits of
science in Lisbon. He ignored me until I gave my talk, about
how no one understands consciousness, including Edelman.
Just a little harmless teasing. But when I glanced down at him,
sitting in the front row in his black undertaker's suit, his skull-
like face was grim. When I walked offstage, he rushed up to
me, eyes blazing, told me I'm a pathetic ignoramus envious of
scientists, trying to drag them down to my subhuman level with
petty foolish insults. Screaming at me in front of everyone. I
nodded along, smiling, thrilled my barbs had hit their mark.

But he was right, I envy him and other discoverers. Oh, to *discover* something! Moons of Jupiter! Radio waves! Electrons! Quarks! Superfluidity! The double helix! Red shift of galaxies! These are discoveries, not *stories*. Any fool can tell a story. What am I compared to Gell-Mann, Crick, Weinberg, Edelman? Or mathematical discoverers like Mandelbrot, who encountered a fantastical N-dimensional attractor on geometry's far frontier. Or inventors like Marconi, Edison, Turing, or the guy who thought up vasectomies. Compared to them I'm nothing. A hack entertainer in a low-status, low-paying sub-niche of show biz. Science journalism, what a joke. Gell-Mann was right, we're parasites.

I tell myself I'm doing good, making the world better by denouncing Bad Science, Bad Ideas. But sometimes I'm just being an asshole, and not only to scientists. I blurt out mean things to friends. Get mad when I'm losing in hockey, yell at teammates, as if their bad passes were moral failings. I love scoring, winning. That's my nature, destiny. After I viciously attacked the Warrior Gene and accused proponents of racism, White Supremacists attacked me, said I probably had the Warrior Gene. I was flattered! I thought, Yeah, I am a Warrior, you Racist Bastards! A Word Warrior!

Probably inherited the Warrior Gene from Dad, along with the Optimism Gene. I'm a walking, talking confirmation of that Evo Psycho idea, what is it? Argumentative Theory. Natural Selection didn't design reasoning skills to discover truth. It designed them to win arguments, make you look smart and your opponent look dumb, impress the ladies, increase reproductive opportunities. Wish I could be nicer, practice Right Speech, like Buddhists. Never say mean things, just write upbeat, entertaining stories about cool scientists discovering and inventing cool things.

Check comments on Free Will column again? Don't be so compulsive. Oh what the Hell, might as well. New comment from PhysicsGuy: *The best response I could come up with to Toole's pathetic defense of free will is the following quote: "If the Moon, in the act of completing its eternal way around the Earth, were gifted with self-consciousness, it would feel thoroughly convinced that it was traveling its way of its own accord…. So would a Being, endowed with higher insight and more perfect intelligence, watching man and his doings, smile about man's illusion that he was acting according to his own Free Will." So who should we believe on free will? Einstein, or a hack journalist like Toole?*

What the…??!! Of *course* the Moon has no Free Will, because unlike me it has no *mind*! I could have called in sick today and spent the day watching *Battlestar Galactica*. I *choose* to teach and write, because I love to. And because if I quit I won't make enough money to support myself, Neal and Claire, and to pick up the tab when Emily and I eat dinner at Gee Whiz. I am free! Within limits.

If Einstein was a Free Will Denier, he was an idiot. Well, maybe not an idiot, just a victim of his ideological commitment to physical determinism. Very Bad Idea. Denouncing Bad Ideas is my duty, destiny, even if it means being an asshole. Fuck Buddhists, fuck Right Speech, just another Bad Idea.

Time? 4:31. Might as well head to the ferry. Stand up. Now? Now? Now? Can feel neurons primed for inevitable decision. Except it's not really a decision, only a matter of timing. So stand up… now! That was my conscious choice, not just the ebb and flow of chemicals in my brain. Oh, give it a rest, you obsessive maniac.

Stuff notebook, laptop and recorder in backpack and pat pants to confirm presence of phone, wallet, keys. How much of life consists of these repetitive chores? If you delete all the stuff we do automatically, like sleeping, eating, excreting, showering, teeth-brushing, commuting, what's left? What part of life actually matters?

Sex, Darwinians would say, because it leads, or used to lead, to reproduction, which is what really matters. But even sex can become automatic. My old pal Frank once confessed sex was beginning to seem pointless. You do it over and over again, he said mournfully, and where does it get you? I didn't know what to tell poor Frank. That's true despair, when sex makes you feel like Sisyphus. Another day, another hump.

Exit Humanities, descend from campus to Hoboken Promenade. Next ferry is... nine minutes. I can make it if I hurry. Here I go, rushing to my death again. Looking down, I see my black Vans striding right, left, right, left over red and gray bricks. The promenade's brickwork goes well beyond basic functionality. It could have been all red bricks, or all gray, but it's made of three alternating strips. Solid red, then red strip with embedded gray square, then solid gray strip, then solid red strip again. Repeat repeat repeat.

The promenade's designer could have added a gray strip with an embedded red square to make the pattern more symmetrical. Or, even cooler, the pattern could have been quasi-periodic, like Conway's Game of Life, or Penrose tiles. Everyone thought Penrose tiles were imaginary, then physicists discovered quasicrystals, three-dimensional versions of Penrose tiles.

We keep finding uncanny correspondences between our fantasies and the world. Like imaginary numbers, made of the square root of negative numbers, which aren't supposed to have square roots. Seemed like a pointless invention, but it turned out to be great for describing quantum weirdness. Is the unreasonable effectiveness of mathematics evidence of divine Platonic order? A Geek God?

Looking down at my feet I realize I'm doing it again, automatically shortening or broadening my stride to land on the edge of one brick strip, cleanly in the middle of the next strip, on the edge of the next. Repeat repeat repeat. Compulsion much worse when I was a kid. I stepped on all the seams of sidewalks or none, counted steps and paving stones, got stuck in infinite loops, like thinking about thinking about thinking. Finding a way out of loops was hard, like trying to remember to forget. Hours later I'd think, Hey, I'm not thinking about thinking any more! Then, Oh no! Repeat repeat repeat. Nasty strange loops taking over my brain.

These loopy programs don't torment me the way they used to. And endless loops aren't so bad if they allow for novelty. They imply that everything comes from an Ur-Algorithm churning out infinite, entropy-defying surprises. What is the Ur-Algorithm, where did it come from? Can we discover it? Imagine it? Escape it? If we can't escape it, does that mean Free Will doesn't exist? The Geek God invented the Ur-Algorithm. If He's watching, He doesn't give a shit about our pain, He just groks the ever-changing patterns.

Cross parking lot to Hoboken Terminal. Terminal's ancient copper façade covered with squirmy bas relief sculptures of…. What are they? Leaves? Fish? Decorations serve no practical purpose except lining pockets of crooked Jersey contractors and politicians. No, too cynical. Civic decorations evidence of the same primordial urge that made our ancestors draw horses and bison on walls of caves. Ladies rewarded talented stone-age artists in the usual Darwinian fashion, so we got the art instinct.

Along with instincts for music, literature, religion, philosophy, science. It's all male competition for females, that's why females are less creative, they can always get laid, don't have to compete for males. That's what Miller says. Evo Psycho is fun, any asshole can do it.

Enter an unmarked side door of the terminal, for workers not commuters. Shortcut saves 15-20 seconds. As I stride down a long dark corridor, lights flick on automatically above me, like they are honoring me. The lights proclaim *Hail, Oh Mighty Philosopher King!* when I'm under them, mutter *Asshole* as soon as I'm past.

Enter the terminal just in time to see a ferry approaching Pier 3. Belching soot, snorting, groaning, the ferry docks, like a fat old man easing into a La-Z-Boy. A horde of passengers disembarks and rushes past me, most of them ogling smartphones. I'm the only passenger to Manhattan, and I don't even own a smartphone, just an old flip phone. I'm special, superior to the herd.

I smugly take a seat in the front row, beside a window, as the ferry churns, pivots, backs up, like Buster Keaton in a silent film, and races across the Hudson. River choppier than usual. The ferry rolls, pitches, bucks but charges inexorably onward, and soon we're nearing the Financial Center Terminal, a mini-mountain range of white tent peaks jutting into the river.

Ferry decelerates, still rolling, pitching. I stand, grab a seat to steady myself. A crowd waits on the pier, staring at smartphones. I cross the gangplank and push through the herd, feeling special again. Our brains seize on every opportunity to bolster our natural narcissism. Like the time I was flying to L.A. and got bumped to first class. When I glimpsed people back in economy through a curtain, they seemed bovine, inferior. I recognize the irrationality of this feeling, but still feel it. We must counteract this terrible tendency by teaching children all are equal and deserving of respect and kindness. Except those who don't treat others with respect and kindness, they must be crushed.

Walk off pier onto land. The pavement rolls and pitches, like I'm still on the ferry. Only eight minutes on the river, and I have sea legs! My balance sensors adjusted to rolling and pitching, and now they need to un-adjust. Like the waterfall illusion. Watch a waterfall for a minute, and your neurons adjust to downward motion. Look away at something stationary, like a tree, and the bark seems to flow upward. Side effect of the brain's plasticity, short-term habituation.

Longer-term habituation can be wrenching. Like when I went to Nicaragua in '85 to see the revolution up close. I lived for a month in Estelí with a Nicaraguan family, Mom and Dad and four kids in a two-room shack. Hose delivered water, electric cord powered a single light bulb, for only an hour or two a day. No refrigerator, no bathroom, just an outhouse, and newspaper for wiping your ass. The stove a brick box that burned wood.

I slept on a cot, and I was grateful, because six family members shared two beds. This life was hard at first, but after a few weeks I got used to it, living in a shack in a town with dirt streets and people who wore ragged clothes and rarely showered. Constant smell of sweat, shit, piss, sound of crying babies and yelling men, women, kids. Distant mortar shells and gunshots at night. My new normal.

Didn't realize how habituated I was until I flew back to Manhattan. Gawked like a bumpkin at skyscrapers of glittering glass and steel, shops crammed with fantastically opulent jewelry and pastries, impeccably coiffed men and women striding up and down avenues in shiny suits and shoes. My shitty studio on East 54th felt like Marie Antoinette's bedroom. My first night home, I felt intense, sensual pleasure as I sat on a flush toilet, took a hot shower, drank water chilled by ice cubes, slipped into clean, smooth sheets on my foldout couch. Manhattan, my home, seemed unreal, dream-like, after just one month away. Within a week, I was re-habituated to skyscrapers, flush toilets, hot showers, ice cream, microwaved tuna melts, clean sheets, sleek women in high heels and lipstick. Now Nicaragua seemed like a dream.

Habituation blinds us to things, good and bad. We get used to our marriage and job, happiness and hardship, poverty and prosperity, war and peace. We no longer see things as they really are. Habituation can help you get through hard times. When my marriage soured I thought, Could be worse. Could be worse. Could *still* be worse. I thought I was doing Tricia a favor hanging in there. Then she ended it. Turned out she hated our marriage more than I did. Funny.

After decades habituated to one woman, suddenly I'm on my own. Single. Dating! Rip Van Winkle wakes up, joins Match.com, starts emailing ladies, chatting over the phone, swapping tales of woe, meeting for coffee, dinner. Then I meet a woman I really like. She looks, sounds, smells, tastes utterly different, utterly unlike Tricia. Calcified networks in the reptilian region of my brain tremble, fissure, sprouting new circuits in response to strange new stimuli from this strange new woman, Emily. Then I habituate to her.

Chapter 6

Pondering the Irish Hunger Memorial

Pause outside the ferry terminal, in Battery Park. Manhattan, home of my Baby. She won't be home for at least another hour. Don't rush to her apartment, don't treat this route as a means to an end. No, Pay Attention, take your time. But what should I Pay Attention to? Trees? Flowers? Pedestrians?

Joggers jog, strollers stroll, commuters rush. So many people! Each a cosmos, parallel universe, packed with infinite details. Impossible to Pay Attention to everything. Brains are reducing valves, Huxley said, and psychedelics open the valve so we see things unfiltered, as they really are. We can see too much, like the Borges character who hit his head, remembered everything, no data compression, no abstraction. He had to lie in a dark room so he wouldn't be overwhelmed by details. What was his name? Fuentes.

Can't see everything, have to be selective. But when we focus on one thing, we miss other things. Like when Christof showed me that video of men and women passing around a basketball and told me to count how many times the ball changes hands. *Seventeen!* I say proudly. Christof smiles and says, That's fine, but did you see the gorilla? Gorilla? I reply. What are you talking about? He plays the video again and there it is, a gorilla strolling, slowly, past the men and women.

How could I be so blind? What else am I missing? Probably all kinds of stuff, because of biases like optimism, faith that things are okay and getting better and better. If I looked at things rationally, I'd get depressed, because I'd have to acknowledge that everything comes down to dumb luck. We're here by accident, could vanish the same way. All our victories are Pyrrhic, tiny triumphs on the road to cold, dead nothingness.

Dyson refuses to accept that, says our descendants can delay Heat Death by becoming super-intelligent, energy-efficient gas clouds. I asked Dyson what a gas cloud would think about, beyond ensuring its own survival. He was stumped. Then his eyes lit up, he said the cloud could work on mathematical problems. Dyson's paradise, drifting through endless space solving math puzzles.

When I mentioned Dyson's vision to Dave, he said Bertrand Russell thought a super-intelligent being would see all mathematics as trivial, tautological, like 1 = 1. So the question remains, What will we think about if we become an immortal, super-intelligent gas cloud? What's worth thinking about for eternity? We'll probably think about what we should think about. I spend more time on that than I care to think about.

Middle-aged guy in a suit passes me, smoking and talking fast. Too fast. "And yeah I texted you and you texted me and I think everything is fine and the next thing I know you're telling me

you have problems with something I said and I'm thinking,
What? I mean, Hey! Ha ha ha. Because everything I told you is
totally one hundred and ten percent true! Ha ha ha." Laughter
so insincere it sounds spoken. A lousy liar, incompetent con
man, can't see how others see him. People probably distrust him
instinctively, because he triggers their lie-detection programs.
I feel bad for him but can't waste compassion on pathetic
sociopaths.

Two tall, skinny guys with rings in ears and noses stroll by
holding hands, exchanging gleeful glances. Taller man crested
by a blond Mohawk, wearing a skintight, short-sleeved shirt
with swirly red-blue-green-yellow images. Wait, that's a tattoo,
covering his whole torso. Not long ago these guys might have
been thrown in jail, beaten, killed. Fearless public affection
of gay men indicates human rights progress, at least in major
metropolitan areas.

Why didn't I ever have sex with a guy? Not even in my nomadic
hitchhiking days, when old guys picked me up and offered me
twenty bucks to suck my dick. Easy money, and I was poor. But
Hyper-vigilant Superego said, No! You're not queer! Adamant,
wouldn't even let me entertain the thought. Because I didn't have
the Gay Gene? No, because I wasn't really a hippy free spirit, I
was a brainwashed goody-goody Catholic boy.

During my Big Drug Trip, I saw The Gorilla. *Became* The Gorilla.
But maybe that Gorilla wasn't real. Maybe the Real Gorilla is
walking past me right now. Not God. Not Death. Something else,
invisible. Stop thinking about that, Pay Attention to the world.
Like the duck pond. Ducks inhabit two worlds, heads and backs
above water, bellies and webbed feet below, with the ghostly
orange goldfish. I watch a black woman watching a white toddler
watching a duck until the woman watches me back.

This breach in the fourth wall unnerves me. Head inland toward a hulking fortress of slate and glass slabs, Irish Hunger Memorial, ringed by a courtyard of black stones with pale crescent-shaped markings, cross sections of ancient shells. Are the fossil-laden stones intended to evoke deep time? Provide a soothing reminder of the transience of human tribulation? Whatever happens, no matter how bad, don't worry about it, this too shall pass, we'll all be dead someday, like these primordial fossilized creatures.

No, the Memorial wants us to remember, *care* about, the Great Hunger that ravaged the land of my ancestors. Inscriptions etched into glass slabs record Ireland's collapse: 4,040,000 people in 1790, 8,175,124 in 1841, down to 5,174,836 in 1881. Brits let the Irish starve but kept great records. Desperation drove Great Grandpa Toole from Ireland to America when he was a lad. Sailed from Dublin to New York City, funneled through Ellis Island, became a builder of slaughterhouses and fire stations, drank himself to death at the dawn of the Great Depression, leaving behind Grandpa Toole, father of my father. If the Brits hadn't been so callous toward the Irish, if the Great Hunger hadn't happened, I wouldn't be standing here looking at the Hunger Memorial. I wouldn't exist.

Should we be thrilled we won a lottery with infinite odds? Or freaked out? Dumb luck gave me this life, dumb luck could take it away, at any moment. That old bastard Gould, guru of contingency, said if you reran the experiment of life on Earth a million times over, each outcome would be utterly different. Evolution depends on randomness, rolls of the dice. You'd never get mammals again, let alone mammals that invent writing, math, science. And science journalism. How random is that? Physics is even more random than biology, it says our world is the culmination of infinite rolls of the dice, starting with the Big

Bang, the roll that got everything rolling. If God exists, He's just the Big Roller, the Holy Roller, with no more idea than we have where we're headed.

Quotes from bigshot human rollers cover the Hunger Memorial walls. Eisenhower: *Every gun that is made, every warship launched, every rocket fired signifies, in the final sense, a theft from those who hunger and are not fed, those who are cold and are not clothed.* Nice speech, Ike, but why did you let Joe McCarthy run amok? Drag us into Vietnam? Make that murderous Quaker Nixon your VP? Sign off on a massive H-bomb buildup? We were one roll of the dice away from annihilation.

Here's Jimmy Carter: *We know that a peaceful world cannot long exist one third rich and two thirds hungry.* Okay, Jimmy, but war begets hunger more than vice versa. Churchill during World War II confiscated so much Indian grain for British troops and civilians that millions of Indians starved. Brits cared even less about Indians than about the Irish.

As I stare at the Hunger Memorial, brooding over humanity's inhumanity, a lithe, tanned woman jogs by in halter top and silky shorts, burning calories to stay fit. Lust curdles into resentment toward her and the suited men and women strolling past me, or sitting at a sidewalk café, sipping martinis and nibbling shrimp. Within eyesight of the Hunger Memorial. Bankers, probably, making millions while others have lousy jobs, lousy schools, homes, health care. Bankers think they're better than the rest of us, because they're richer, but they're worse. They're bad people.

Wait. Analyze the issue calmly, rationally, without emotion, the way Singer would. Give capitalism credit for growing global prosperity, decline of poverty. Huge step forward for humanity, along with longer life, more democracy, less war. Things are getting better! And bankers aren't all bad. My fellow Tooles, Dad and Matt, are bankers, and they're good guys. Bankers with Irish blood probably put up the bucks for this lovely Hunger Memorial.

Singer would probably say, Instead of wasting money remembering the dead, help people starving *now*. Singer good at laying guilt trips on us. Imagine walking through a park, you see a kid drowning in a pond. You're wearing brand-new shoes, no time to take them off. Do you let the kid drown? Of course not. You jump in, save the kid, ruin your shoes. Only a monster would keep walking. Then Singer springs his Gotcha. If you spend money on fancy clothes, cars, TVs, restaurants, vacations, stuff you don't really need, you're a monster, because you could spend that money saving starving third-world kids.

Singer's argument made me feel so guilty that I grasped for counterarguments. Yes, I have $100 running shoes, and a big-screen TV. But I don't eat out much, usually wear jeans and t-shirts, drive an old Prius. I am responsible for Neal and Claire, carriers of my genes, must save money for them. Can't give it away to strangers, however poor. And I should get moral credit for writing, albeit rarely, about inequality…

Weak. Here's another argument. You are responsible for your own happiness. Can't let humanity's suffering keep you from enjoying your life. Pity can become pathology. Look at Simone Weil, starved herself to death to protest atrocities of World War II. What good did that do anyone, Simone? People suffer and die, life and pursuit of happiness must go on. Like Bruegel's painting of Icarus. He's tumbling into the sea, drowning, and no one notices. As it should be.

What good do Do Gooders do, really? Like those activists I met at the antiwar rally, did serious jail time, a year or more, for breaking into drone plants and missile sites. They arranged in advance for friends to take care of their kids. I told them I admired their courage and commitment. But I thought, I would never abandon my kids for a cause, and what did your protests accomplish?

Do Gooders just rolling the dice. Even the noblest memes, once they start spreading, mutate into something ugly. Christ's message of love inspires Crusades and the Inquisition. Marx's vision of equality and justice leads to the Gulag. Who will save us from our saviors? Tend your own garden, don't try to terraform the planet.

Rationalizing, because I'm too lazy, selfish, cowardly to sacrifice my creature comforts, let alone my life, for an idea. Like that fight I had with Mom when I graduated from high school. She was afraid I'd get a high number in the draft lottery, get sent to Vietnam. I said, Don't worry Mom, I'll leave the country if I'm drafted. Mom frowned and said, If you think war is wrong, you should defy the law and face the consequences, running away is cowardly. I said, Are you nuts? Prison would be worse than the Army!

Poor Mom, she wanted her son to be a brave idealist, not a lazy, cowardly stoner. I should visit her grave, apologize for all the shit I put her through.

Bring, bring. Neal! He never calls, hope everything is okay.

"Neal! What a surprise!"

"Hey Dad." Voice calm as always. Neal's cool, unlike his father.

"How are you? What's up?"

"I'm okay. But, uh, actually, I need money. My meal plan is running low."

"Oh, sure, no problem. I'll deposit a few hundred bucks in your bank account tonight."

"Thanks Dad, talk to you later."

"Wait! Come on, Neal, I never get to talk to you. Tell me how you're doing. Are you enjoying school more?"

"I guess. I don't know."

"Okay, that doesn't sound good. Are you still thinking about, you know…?"

"Yeah, actually, I've done a little more research. I was thinking about the Marines at first, but now I realize that's for guys who are gung-ho about combat. The Army would probably be a better match for me. It has some cool-looking programs."

"Like what?"

"Well, there's something called explosive ordnance disposal that looks pretty interesting."

"Explosive ordnance disposal? Is that… getting rid of bombs? Like *The Hurt Locker*?"

"Yeah, but the guy in *The Hurt Locker* was crazy. Ordnance disposal is actually not that dangerous if you do it right. It requires a lot of specialized training, in chemistry, electronics, stuff like that."

Don't say it. "Jesus, Neal." Can't stop myself. "Are you trying to torture me?" I hear through the phone a muffled female voice saying something, and Neal's muffled voice responding.

"Dad, sorry, I've gotta go. Thanks for taking care of the meal plan."

"Neal, if you become a soldier, I know you'll be a good one. But please, *please* stay in college. At least finish the semester."

"Okay, Dad." Humoring the Old Man. "Bye."

Shit! I've been brainwashing him since he was tiny, telling him War is Bad. Freedom, choices, options good. And now here he is, thinking about becoming a soldier, freely giving up his freedom. My son, a warrior. Ironic. Also ironic that part of me likes imagining Neal in a clean, crisp uniform, fit, clear-eyed, manly, sitting in a classroom with other young, uniformed men and women with excellent posture, earnestly taking notes on a plastic explosives lecture. I'd be proud, not ashamed. Better a soldier than a hippy bum like I was at his age.

A few weeks ago, after Neal said college felt pointless, I said, Being a soldier is worse than pointless, because killing people is the point. He grimaced and said, Dad, I don't want to kill people. I want to help people, protect people, soldiers do that too. He's right. Made me feel like a self-righteous old fool. Neal's always thoughtful, a good boy. I wanted him to be meaner sometimes. Fantasized about him punching bullies in school, crushing opponents in lacrosse games. But Neal's not hotheaded and mean like me. He'll make a fine soldier. Peacekeeper. Even in a world without war, we'll need soldiers to protect us from violent sociopaths, apocalyptic suicidal cults. To keep peace. Defuse bombs. Feed starving kids. Brave, calm, kind men like Neal. Women too.

Head away from the Hunger Memorial envisioning Neal marching at the front of a Peacekeeper Army. Attractive young men and women and transgenders of all ethnicities wearing uniforms with peace signs over their hearts. Armed with phasers set to stun.

Walking on Warren toward West Street, I confront an enormous, Seurat-like tableau. Scores of girls and boys in multicolored shorts and shirts chase balls on an emerald field punctuated by blue and white stripes, yellow cones and nets. Men in business suits yell, Run! Run! Pass! Shoot! Good! A woman in a slinky silver cocktail sheath kicks a ball back and forth with a purple-uniformed boy. She claps her hands and shouts, Yeah, yeah! Busy, successful men and women taking time to coach their kids, help them excel, so they'll grow up to be busy, successful men and women. Repeat, repeat.

Did I do enough for Neal and Claire? I tried. Bought a lacrosse stick and net for Neal, played catch in the yard, practiced offense, defense, shooting when he came home from school. That lasted, what, a month or two? I tried to teach Claire to ski when she was seven or eight. Took her on a slope much too steep, she fell on her face, walked down the rest of the way, never skied again. She never forgot, keeps reminding me how much that day traumatized her.

Tricia calls me a lousy father. Stings because there's truth to it. But you can be a great parent and your kid ends up dumb, disabled, depressed. Or mean. What's worse? Your kid becoming a gentle, sad failure or a joyful sociopath? Tough choice. I'd probably go with sociopath. You want your kid to be happy, right? Even if he makes others unhappy.

My faith in Free Will, progress, human improvability makes me viciously attack scientists who say genes are destiny. Like Hamer, Watson, Minnesota Twin researchers. I hate stories about twins separated at birth who both turn out to be firefighters who drink Budweiser, marry women named Linda, name their dogs Toy. Right, there's a gene for calling a puppy Toy, or liking girls named Linda. Stupid Gene Whiz Science.

But more truth in bio-determinism than I like to admit. Neal was always into swords, guns, first-person shooter games, paintball. Started talking about being a soldier when he was 13, 14. I asked him, joking, not joking, how a peacenik like me had a son like him. He reminded me my father and grandfather were soldiers, Navy men, both fought in World War II. I'm the oddball, not him. Smart boy.

There's an upside to genetic determinism. If your kid messes up, it's not your fault, the dice just didn't roll your way. Some kids are born bad. Mike and Mindy, wonderful people, doted on Kendra, and she became a junkie by 15. Mike and Mindy blew their savings on swank rehab centers, in vain. Took Kendra home, she stole from them, brought strange men into the house, overdosed in her bedroom when she was 19. What would Singer do if his daughter got hooked on heroin? Spend $50,000 on rehab when she'll probably relapse anyway? Or send money to Oxfam to save hundreds of sick, hungry kids? Plug that into your utilitarian calculator, Singer.

Mom blamed herself when I blew off college and became a bum, roaming around the country. But it was all my fault. My chemistry, my genes, made me choose my stupid path. At least she lived long enough to see me finish college and grad school and become a science writer. A miracle! Then she got the headaches and nausea, and X-rays showed a tumor in her brain.

Lying in a hospital before her operation, she told me she had a good life, a good marriage, five good healthy children. What more could anyone want? She was at peace, ready to die. I wish she could have been alive when my first book was published. I wish she could have met Emily.

The woman in the slinky silver dress has stopped kicking the ball with her son. She's staring at me. She digs me. No, she thinks I'm a creep checking out kids in shorts. Time to move.

Crossing West Street, I watch the light on the far corner count down seconds: 16, 15, 14… Tech innovation making the world safer, better. Signs of hope everywhere if you look, hope based on measurable, material trends. Not delusional. Yeah, more than a billion people starving, sick, with no clean water, no schools, no medicine, and thousands of homeless mentally ill people right here in New York, living on the streets. But check out these cool signs for pedestrians!

Human progress is a joke, we keep slamming into obstacles we put in our own path.

Stop in Whole Foods? Buy her a treat? Raisins covered in white chocolate! Hilarious! A little joke, make us both laugh about that silly fight last week. No, better not, could backfire. What was I thinking, Bad Idea.

Head down Warren, left on Greenwich, past Soft Ice Cream truck. Ice Cream Man leans out of the window, arms folded on the counter. Ironic contrast between his mournful, bulldog face and the colorful images on his truck. Popsicles, sundaes, swirly ice cream cones with multicolored sprinkles. Look at Ice Cream Man, Pay Attention. Poor guy.

Ice Cream Man looks straight back at me with sad saggy eyes, startling me. A breach of protocol, privacy. We're peering into each other's souls, seeing each other naked. Look away! For weeks after my Big Drug Trip I felt oneness with others, Thou Art That, but it wasn't blissful. When I passed strangers on the street, a blue-white current streamed from their eyes into mine, binding our souls together in an electric loop. The world wobbled, like a reflection in a pool. Part of me thought, I'm just hallucinating, I've got a bad case of derealization. Another part believed, *knew* I was seeing Things As They Really Are. None of us is real, we're all figments of God's imagination. We're God's confabulations.

I get flashbacks now and then, but I choose to ignore them, embrace *Maya*, live in the world of illusion. I am real, Ice Cream Man is real. Emily, Neal, Claire, my students and colleagues are real. Thou Art Not That. I am not you. I can't be a father, teacher, boyfriend and also a mystic. How can I love Emily if she isn't real? How can she love me?

During my Big Drug Trip I saw with mathematical clarity two primal forces, attraction and repulsion, interpenetrating arrows, ropes in a braid, sides of a Möbius strip. Repulsion as well as attraction makes the world go round. If love were the only cosmic force, we'd collapse into a black hole, into oblivion. But maybe I wasn't seeing The Way Things Are. Maybe I was just seeing The Coldness in me.

I rationalize, tell myself everyone is cold. Love fades, we stay together for other reasons. Avoidance of loneliness. Mutual ego stroking. Conforming to expectations of friends, family. Expense sharing. Convenience. Emily jokes, You don't love me, you love Hotel Emily! Her apartment twice the size of mine, half an hour from my office, saves me a long commute. I say, Yeah, Baby, and

I dig your room service! But her joke about Hotel Emily isn't a joke. When she talks about The Coldness, I say, I'm not cold, Baby, I'm hot for you! But it stings.

The Coldness helped me get through the end of my marriage. No matter how bad things got, Tricia crying or screaming, part of me was just watching. Like a guy sitting alone in a movie theater thinking, *Interesting.* When I broke up with Emily, dumped her, and she started crying, part of me felt bad, reached out, rubbed her back, muttered, I'm sorry. Another part watched her, thinking, *Interesting.* Buddhists spend years meditating to achieve The Coldness. I was born with it.

Bring, bring. Emily!

"I was just thinking about you, Baby!"

"Of course you were, Poodle Butt," she says.

She keeps inventing new nicknames for me. When I try to reciprocate, my attempts fall flat. I call her Chicken Breast or Sticky Bun, as if she reminds me of food. When she's being especially bossy, I bow and scrape and call her Mistress Emily. Passive aggressive. I usually stick to Baby. "I'm almost at your apartment. Where are you?"

She talks rapidly, even more than usual, over background noise. Bus? Jackhammer? I hear her say "leaving work," "subway," "dinner." Okay, got it. She just left work, wants me to meet her at the Chambers subway station. We'll eat dinner nearby.

"All right, see you soon, Baby."

Fondness floods me, memories of when we met, after I left Tricia and moved into my own place. I was lonely, aching, didn't expect love, or even sex, just wanted a little affection. Then I spotted her beaming face on Match.com. She looked kind. I was a year or two above her age range but figured I'd give her a shot. Her profile said she was in publishing, so I sent her a message: I'm in publishing too, I'm a writer! She wrote back, we chatted over the phone, talked about whether e-books were good or bad for writers. She sounded smart, brisk, professional, which worried me. Agreed to meet me after work at a cafe near her midtown office.

She looked too corporate, young, pretty for an old hippy like me. I expected a short, awkward encounter, but we yakked about internet dating, books, science, psychiatry, spirituality, until I realized how late it was. I had to catch the train to Cold Spring. She walked me 10 blocks to Times Square, hugged me goodbye at the subway entrance. I barely made the train, stared out the window all the way home, not even seeing the Hudson, replaying scenes from my encounter with this strange new creature, imagining future scenes. I ran from the Cold Spring station up Main and down Fair to my apartment composing romantic notes, to make her want to see me again. I flipped open my laptop and found an email from her waiting for me: *I hope you made your train! xoxo, Emily.* My heart went, *Ping!*

Those first few months I was in a fever state of heightened attention. Everything looked bright, shiny, magical. I felt so happy, *joyful*, that I thought a mistake had been made. Fate would soon correct the error, adjust reality in accordance with Conservation of Misery. I was extra careful crossing streets, worried that a cab or bus, an Agent of Fate, would run me over. Then I thought, This is natural, fated, meant to be. I'm *blessed! Chosen!* Love felt biochemical, uncontrollable, almost as much as depression. The feeling faded, gave way to habituation, doubts, second-guessing. The Dumping. Then I won her back. Now I *choose* to be with her, because she makes me happier, healthier, nicer. Without her I'd be lost, a sad old grouch sitting alone in a dark theater waiting for the movie of his life to end.

Men in grimy orange vests and yellow hardhats stand around a hole in front of the Verizon store. Greenwich Street's asphalt skin has been ripped away, exposing ancient, encrusted, rotted pipes and cables, the city's bowels, conveying water, shit, piss, toilet paper, electrons and photons beneath the streets. Urban entrails can be repaired, replaced, in defiance of the Second Law. Unlike my organs, which decay irreversibly. Will we defeat senescence some day? Will stem cells, genetic tweaks regenerate bodies like cities? Billionaires are funding life-extension research, but Steve Jobs is still dead. Emily has delayed my decay, even reversed it, temporarily. If we live together, will I become habituated to her again? No. She won't let that happen. I won't let it happen. I will never stop Paying Attention to her.

Chapter 7

Meeting Emily

Cross Greenwich, stride east on Chambers, through a throng
of backpacked, gabbing, texting community college kids in
front of McDonald's. Our future in their hands, and that's okay,
smart decent young people will save the world! Pass PetSmart,
Subway, Marine Corps Career Center. Two buzz-cut uniformed
young men loitering at the entrance, like hookers trolling for
customers, kids who don't know what to do, like Neal. No, Neal
is sensible, he would only enlist after careful weighing of pros
and cons, but please don't become like the guy in *Hurt Locker*.

Arrive at subway entrance northeast corner of Chambers and
West Broadway. Lean against subway elevator, half hidden so I
can see her coming up the stairs without her seeing me. I'll creep
up behind her, grab her butt, make her yelp. She hates that,
loves it.

Commuters descend stairs randomly, ascend nonrandomly in
clusters, as subways below me disgorge. Most people trudge,

some trot, eager, for what? Dates, cocktails, dinner, plays. Kinky sexual trysts. Yoga, meditation, jogging. Hanging with spouses, kids, pets. Or being alone, reading magazines, books, gambling on the internet, watching news, porn, Netflix. Maybe they'll sprawl on a tattered couch watching *Battlestar Galactica*, like me when I'm not with her. The things we do while rushing to our death.

Here she comes! No, just looks like Emily. Similar height, hair, clothes. Actually, not at all similar. Too skinny, too much makeup, hint of henna in the hair. There I go again, Mr. Magoo, mistaking one thing for another. False positive from the neural loop dedicated to her, the Emily Loop, which encodes countless memories. Emily doing the twist in a new yellow bikini. Scrutinizing an orange pepper in Whole Foods. Sitting across from me at Gee Whiz slicing eggs Florentine. Lying in bed holding my hand as we watch *Girls*.

Emily Loop will flash like plugged-in Christmas lights when she appears, dark hair framing her pale, stoic street face. Someday optogenetic implants will sense, decode, transmit neural chatter for mutual mind-reading, telepathic communication. Could help me solve the Birthday Present Problem. She yearns for a gift revealing my deep love and knowledge of her, but her tastes are quirky, and she buys what she wants for herself after exhaustive online research. My gifts invariably disappoint her. Not as bad as raisins dipped in white chocolate, but still.

After the Singularity, my implant will query hers and select the perfect gift. But will she be surprised? Grateful? Will Valentine's Day survive the Singularity? Only if implants give us the option of keeping secrets from each other, even from ourselves. Yeah, privacy perpetuates miscommunication, deception, self-deception, but the price is worth paying for romance. National

Security Agency will insist on a backdoor privacy-override. Let them have it, I don't care, as long as Emily remains a mystery to me.

Emily Loop represents the essence of her, the Platonic ideal, which transcends all details, specific memories, fantasies. I should make her part of my Pay Attention project. Start tonight, record conversation with her about important topics. Record me asking The Question, her answering. If I ask.

6:27. Where the hell is she? Been here 20 minutes at least. Subway malfunction? Police foiling terrorist plot? Is she stuck between stations? Could call her but no point, no reception down there. I couldn't have missed her, could I?

Bring, bring. Emily! Fantastically complex chain of events precedes appearance of letters on my flip phone. Begins with neural activity in her brain, leading to thought, decision, action, finger motions—digital activity!—transformed by her phone into microwave signals leaping through space at speed of light to my phone, which processes signals instantly interpreted by my brain. Amazing!

"Honey, where are you?" Her voice conveys concern. Or annoyance.

"I'm waiting for you, Baby!"

"Where?"

"At the subway, Chambers and Broadway, like you said."

"I told you to meet me at Subway! The sandwich place!" Definitely annoyance.

"What?! I could have sworn you said… I thought you wanted me to meet you at the subway entrance. Like the other time."

"I waited for you in Subway for 15 minutes."

"So where are you now?"

"I'm home."

"Do you still want to go out to dinner? We could meet at Gee Whiz."

"No, I already bought a sandwich from Subway."

"What am I going to do for dinner?"

"You do whatever you like, Mr. Magoo."

"Ha ha. Okay, Baby, I'll get a sandwich from Subway too. See you soon."

Not how I expected our reunion to unfold. The fallibility of language! Will implants eliminate that, or just lead to new forms of miscommunication? Hustle back down Chambers and enter Subway. So many choices! Choose Meatball Marinara. But what size? Bread? Cheese? Toppings? Dressing? Toasted or not? Twelve inches too much, six not enough, like boners. Too many options can lead to indecision, paralysis, apathy. Freedom so hard, leads inevitably to mistakes, even calamities. But what's the alternative? Each choice will take me on a different trajectory, world-path. I feel shadowy quantum doppelgängers branching off into countless other worlds and ordering different subs.

"Your girlfriend was here," says the guy behind the counter. "Waiting for you." Lovely lilting accent. From Ivory Coast, he once told me. Married, with a son.

"I know. I messed up. I thought she wanted to meet me at the subway stop, but she meant here."

He smiles, nods. "Honest mistake."

"Yeah. She was a little upset. But I'll make it up to her." We smile at each other, conveying timeless, wordless, heterosexual, man-to-man message. Women, right? Yeah, Women. Looks too young, carefree to have a wife and kid.

Louis yanks open the door to Emily's building before I get to it. "Hi Louis." "Hi Eamon." Doormen are weird relics of the master-servant era, *Upstairs, Downstairs*. After our breakup… After The Dumping, Emily ordered her doormen not to let me in any more. When she took me back, rescinded her order, I imagined the doormen thinking, She could do better than this jerk.

Exit elevator, slip key into Emily's door. It opens, magically, like that Updike story about a guy who smokes pot at a Manhattan party, takes a cab back to his apartment, feels astonished when the key opens the door, as though he's solved an extremely complex mathematical puzzle. Updike makes the mundane marvelous, sparkly with hi-def detail. Everything *is* marvelous, if we Pay Attention.

Enter her apartment with 12-inch Meatball Marinara Sub. Feel… anticipation? Anxiety? Touch of stage fright? Hissing noise, Emily in the kitchen making seltzer with her Penguin machine. Still wearing sensible work clothes, jeans, gray t-shirt, loafers. She likes to blend into the background, wear dull plumage, like a female finch. No makeup. Tiny gold earrings, thin gold necklace barely visible against her ivory skin. No other adornment. With slightly forced cheerfulness I say, "Finally!" Bending my face to hers, I watch her lick her upper lip. It's wet when we kiss. I love it when she does that.

She pours fizzy seltzer into a glass. "I still don't understand how you went to the subway station. Weren't you listening to me?"

"Yeah, sorry about that. I misheard you, there was a lot of street noise. So how was your day?" She sips seltzer, talks about her boss, deal they're working on, based on a book she likes, she's not positive it'll make a good movie, but definite potential. Unloading my backpack, I nod and say, "Mmm hmmm." Willfully attentive, listening, being a Good Boyfriend, making up for Subway error. Honest mistake, but Mr. Magoo-ish, hate reinforcing that image.

Circle arms around her waist. "I missed you today!" I say, and realize I mean it. She hugs me back, briefly, twists away, flips through mail. I always imagine her soft and yielding before reunions, but she's usually prickly. She's not mad, is she? Not the time to ask The Question. Tell her about Pay Attention Project?

"I think I know what my next book is going to be about." I tell her about taking notes all day, recording class and lunch with colleagues, for stream-of-thought account of a day in a science guy's life.

She looks at me with dismay. "Oh, Honey. No one will want to read that."

I don't need brain implants to know what she's thinking. She tells me. Blunt. "Maybe not. But I want to write it. And actually, I'd like to record us talking tonight. Maybe while we're eating dinner. Would that be okay?"

Sighs, examines mail again. "If it makes you happy."

"Great! Are you hungry? Because I'm starving. I'm gonna eat my meatball sub right now, the Whole Schmagoogle."

"Schmagoogle?"

"Yeah. It's a Yiddish word."

"No, it's not. You're probably thinking of *schmegegge*. It means dumbbell, like a certain boyfriend." She taps her finger against my forehead. She must be right, her father spoke Yiddish. Jim was goofing on me and I fell for it! Leaving the kitchen she says, "You can eat in the bedroom if you use a plate, and you're careful. I'll be in in a minute." My blunt, bossy girlfriend.

Put meatball sandwich on plate, walk into bedroom, strip down to boxers and t-shirt, stretch out on bed with plate on lap. Unwrap sandwich carefully. Eating on her bed a privilege. Get sauce on her duvet and she'll revoke the privilege, banish me to the kitchen. Where is she? In her bathroom. Don't be impatient. She has no patience for my impatience.

Grab *Time Out* from bedside table, turn to sex column, on origins of non-reproductive sex. "Is There an Oral Sex Instinct?" Good question. Did hunter-gatherers lick pussy? Suck dick? Probably. Bonobos lick each other, so oral sex must be innate, not learned. Remember Evo Psycho powwow in Santa Barbara, beach party after day of lectures, Darwinians drinking beers around a bonfire, arguing about origins of romance, male chivalry toward females. Ancient genetic trait or modern cultural invention? Someone said, Hey Roger, you lived with the !Kung. Were the men romantic lovers or just wham-bam-thank-you-ma'am? Roger smiled and said, Well, I can tell you this. A man who knows how to give !Kung women pleasure will enjoy many reproductive opportunities. Ho ho ho, the Evo Psychos loved that.

Romantic love *must* have deep roots. Love much more intense, consuming than lust. Sex quenches lust, makes love burn hotter. The first rush of love feels feverish, obsessive, a loopy program infecting your brain. You can't stop thinking about someone, desiring someone, even if you know rationally that this person is bad for you. You have no choice.

Some people still have mates chosen for them, like girls in Afghanistan. Or the ex-Moonie in my men's group, Dorian, a filmmaker. Six of us gray-haired guys met first Saturday of the month in a Cold Spring church to bitch about wives, ex-wives, girlfriends, kids, careers. Dorian got married decades ago in Madison Square Garden to a girl he'd never met, picked for him by Reverend Moon. Dorian quit the Moonies but still remembered Moon fondly, called him The Rev. No regrets. Other guys in the men's group came to complain, Dorian just wanted to hang out, swap stories. He had the happiest marriage in our men's group by far. Arranged, not his choice, or his wife's. What does that say about Free Will?

Come on, she's taking too long. "My meatballs are getting cold!"

"I said don't wait for me! Why don't you Google yourself or something."

"Ha ha." Her teasing is charming, annoying. Don't react, just observe. Pay Attention. On the wall to my left hang two charcoal sketches of Emily nuzzling a dog. Drawn by her ex-husband Dwayne, an artist. Emily ended the marriage after the romance faded, more than a decade ago. They love each other like brother and sister now, talk over the phone almost every day. She flies to Los Angeles every summer to see him. She has love to spare. Tricia and I haven't spoken in more than a year. Is that my fault?

Be patient. Be patient. "What are you doing in there?"

Toilet flushes, heralding her entry into the bedroom. She walks past me holding her veggie sandwich on a plate, wearing blue panties and a pink t-shirt, nipples faintly visible through thin fabric. "What did you think I was doing?" she says. "Bedazzling my vagina?"

"I don't know what that means, but I'm intrigued."

"It's this thing women are doing now. They glue these little rhinestones on their body, including their private parts."

"I've learned something new today."

She sits on the bed beside me with her plate in her lap, lifts the sandwich, nips one corner off with her delicate rosy mouth. Male-female sex thing so mysterious. For billions of years, nothing but single-celled organisms, no girl or boy bacteria. Then sex happened. Who ordered that? The Geek God? Who knows, but Good Idea. Fantastic Idea! Like a really fruitful mathematical axiom, algorithm, from which endless surprises flow. Glad I live in a sexy world. Sure, sex causes jealousy, hatred, violence, spreads disease, undermines reason, but a fantastic plot device, best McGuffin ever. Hard to believe sex just an accident. Best evidence for divine creation.

Grab digital recorder, hit RECORD, set it on the bed between us. "Here we go, Baby. We're live!"

"Oh, for God's sake. I'm only agreeing to this because you're never going to write this book. And if you do, no one will ever read it."

"You'll have to read it to find out what I really think about."

"Oh, I know what you think about, Monkey Man."

"That's not all I think about. So I'd like to start by asking you about Free Will."

Sighing. "Why?"

"I'm obsessed with it, as you know. And I realize I have no idea what you think about it." I want to know, I don't want to know. I bite my meatball sandwich, and a droplet of red sauce dribbles onto my t-shirt. Grab napkin, wipe sauce off before she sees.

"I saw that!"

"Don't worry, I didn't get any on the bed. Okay, enough stalling. What do you think about Free Will?"

"Why do you care so much about it?"

"Because some scientists say we don't really have any choices in life. Everything is fated, our sense of being able to control our lives by exercising Free Will is an illusion."

"Honey, this is a silly philosophical debate, it's a waste of time to worry about it."

Gulp down chunk of meatball, shaking my head. "Worrying about that stuff is my career! And it's not just some abstract philosophical thing, it's important! If we stop believing in Free Will, we might become passive and fatalistic. Life becomes this thing that happens to us, instead of something we're responsible for."

She chews thoughtfully, swallows. "Sometimes we're better off accepting things that happen to us, if we can't do anything about them. You know what I think is really smart? That thing that people in Alcoholics Anonymous say, about having the wisdom to know the difference between what you can and can't control."

"Yeah, of course there are things we can't control, we can't change. But there are lots of things we *can* change—*if* we believe we can change them. I quit drinking because I wanted to do it, and I believed I could do it, because I have Free Will." If I hadn't met teetotaling Emily, I'd still be drinking. In other universes, where I never met her, or she didn't like me, my doppelgängers are sad old drunks.

"I definitely believe in willpower," she says. "You know, strength of character. Some people have the strength to fight adversity, and they can inspire the rest of us to be strong when terrible things happen, like getting cancer." She leans toward her bedside table, raps her knuckles against it. Superstitious Emily. "And other people just lie down. They give up. And I don't mean that in a judgmental way. Some people just have more of that strength than others. A lot of it comes down to chemistry and genes and things like that."

Talking about herself? Depressed through her teens, twenties, then pulled herself out of it through sheer determination. She's stronger than me, and wiser. Is that what bothers me? "But just because *some* people don't have choices doesn't mean *no one* has choices," I say. "I have more choices than someone with severe depression, or schizophrenia, or a brain tumor. I have more choices than a girl in Afghanistan who's forced to marry some old guy she doesn't even know and become a baby factory. Or a young black guy in this country who gets busted for weed and ends up in prison. Free Will must exist if some people have more of it than others." My slam dunk argument. Who could disagree?

She says, as if speaking to a dim child, "Honey, being born white and male and privileged in America has nothing to do with Free Will. That's luck too, just like brain chemistry."

Frustrating, we're talking past each other, miscommunicating. Why can't she see things as I do? "Yeah, there's always luck involved. But we can also change our luck by the choices we make. We can change our lives, so we have more choices, more freedom. But we have to believe in our power to do that, or we won't even try."

She purses her lips, nods slightly. "Okay, I think I understand you. And I can see how science maybe is related. Science can help us find out what we can and can't control. And science can also give us more control over certain things, like diabetes. We haven't found a cure for it, but now we have a delivery system for insulin so people with diabetes can have long, healthy lives. And maybe science can invent better drugs for depression, so we don't just give up."

"I like that, except you're still making it sound like everything comes down to chemistry and other physical factors. I'm talking about psychology, the mind, consciousness. You look at your life, at where you are now and where you want to go, and you realize you have options. You weigh the pros and cons of different options, and you choose the best one, based on a careful, rational assessment. That's Free Will."

"Rationality is overrated. Especially *your* rationality, Mr. Magoo. When I make decisions, I do research, and get as much information as I can, and I try to make a smart decision. I use common sense, but I also use my Intuition."

"Uh oh. Not..."—wave my hands in the air and say portentously, like a magician chanting a spell—"*In-tu-i-tion!*" One of our rituals. She defends Intuition, I mock it.

"Yes, Mr. Science Man, Intuition. Just because your science doesn't understand it doesn't mean it's not real."

"You mean using Tarot cards and all that stuff? To help you make decisions? To me that's giving away your choices. It reminds me of this novel I read a long time ago, called *Dice Man*. It's about this cult of people who make all their decisions by rolling dice. The cult leader says giving up your choices, leaving them up to chance, gives you real freedom. Interesting idea, very Buddhist. But total fucking bullshit."

"I know people who use Tarot for making all their decisions. Even little ones, like buying a sweater. But that's an abuse of it. The whole point of Tarot and all fortune telling is to develop your Intuition and eventually lay those tools aside. Because they just reveal what you already know, in your gut."

"My gut is extremely intelligent. It told me to buy this meatball sandwich, which is delicious." I hold my sandwich up like a sacrament. Why am I so goofy with her? What's the point? To remind her and me that life isn't just terrifying and heartbreaking, it's silly, funny, Good and Evil reconciled in a laugh.

Emily, not laughing: "Sometimes people get confused about how they feel, and fortune telling can help them figure it out. That's something I learned when I took a Tarot class, and the teacher made us do readings at psychic fairs. Most of the people who want readings are women with questions about love. A lot of them ask, Is my husband or boyfriend cheating on me? Usually the cards are very definite, whether he's cheating or not. And when I tell them, women usually say, Yeah, I had a feeling, that's why I asked."

"Yeah," I say, "but Intuition can be wrong. Maybe this woman is just the jealous type, and her husband isn't actually cheating on her. Maybe you're giving her wrong information."

"It's not like that. When you're telling someone's fortune, you don't just say, Yes, your husband is cheating on you. Next! You ask, Well, what do you want to *do* about this? How do you *feel* about this? So people leave the table with something helpful. Every good fortune teller is a little like a psychotherapist."

"Yeah, and every psychotherapist is just a fortune teller," I say. Another ritual, my disparagement of psychotherapy, which helped her in the past. "So fortune telling is just discovering things that you know on some level? Things that are in your subconscious? It doesn't involve anything supernatural?"

"What do you mean by supernatural?" she asks.

"You know, things that science says are impossible. Like ESP, or ghosts, or miracles. God curing a little girl with cancer because her parents prayed for her."

"Honey, you know I don't believe in God. If that's what you mean by supernatural, then Intuition and fortune telling aren't supernatural. But I do believe that we're all connected, energetically, and that can lead to very powerful Intuitions. Like if I wake up in the middle of the night and see my father, and then I find out that at exactly that time he died far away."

Spooky action at a distance. "You never told me that happened to you."

"It didn't," she says. "But it's happened to people I know, and I totally believe them. There are some Intuitions that are *not* easily explained by science."

"I talked about ESP in class today. A lot of my students believe in it. Some prominent scientists do too. But there's no evidence."

"Honey, you should write a book about scientists who believe in ESP. That's a book people might actually read. That's a book that *I* might read." Sensible Emily, publishing executive, wants me to write books that will make money. So do I!

"If I wrote the book, you wouldn't like it," I say. "I'd have to say what I believe, that even really smart, rational people can brainwash themselves into believing in things that aren't real. Like ghosts, and ESP, and a God who loves us. We're all subject to confirmation bias, and wishful thinking. Science helps us overcome flaws in our thinking that make us prone to superstitious beliefs. Although of course science is far from foolproof."

"For me, Intuition is often more reliable than the intellect," she replies. "The intellect can play tricks on you. People use logic all the time to talk themselves into bad decisions." She dabs a napkin across her mouth and looks at me sternly. "After The Dumping, my cards told me that you still loved me, in spite of what you did, and you would come back to me. I told my closest friends, and they all said I was kidding myself. They said you were an asshole, and that I should forget about you and start dating other guys. So that's what I did. But the cards were right. My *Intuition* was right." She smiles. "Of course, my friends were right too, you *were* an asshole."

I smile weakly. The Dumping is a conversation killer. We've finished our sandwiches. Emily reaches over to her bedside table, grabs her turquoise cat-eye glasses and a book she's been reading on medieval magic. I stack her plate on mine and go into the kitchen. Sweep wrappers, napkins, crumbs into the garbage pail, wash plates, put them in the dish rack, thinking about her bluntness, bossiness, prickliness. She's so stubbornly herself. Is this going to work?

Before returning to the bedroom, I pause in the living room. Pay Attention. She collects things, which sit on tables and shelves. Boxes made of wood, brass, porcelain, glass, intricately carved, etched, painted. Clear and cloudy crystal balls mounted on tripods. Carved wooden men with mother-of-pearl eyes, tongues hanging down, penises sticking up. Where did she get this stuff? I have no idea, never asked her. To me they are pointless, things that take up space, collect dust. She hates it when I call them knickknacks. They give her pleasure, they are rainbow-hued sprinkles on the ice cream cone of her life. A bookcase running the length of the room is crammed with books on Astrology, Tarot, Kabbalah, Alchemy, Witchcraft, Palmistry, Tantra, Freemasonry. The Whole Occult Schmagoogle. Intuition Tools. On a low shelf stand two of my books, nerdy uptight geeks at a rave.

Belief has power, for ill or good. If you think life is pointless, a gradual, painful slide toward dissolution, your belief will be self-fulfilling. If you see magic and meaning and beauty in the world, it will become magical and meaningful and beautiful. If you believe love awaits you, you have a better chance of finding it. Her Intuition told her this a long time ago. She had an absent father and cruel mother, spent her youth in darkness, willed herself to become a happy loving person, a witch with magical powers. She cast a spell on a sad old man, made him feel young and happy. Not a trick, real magic. I have no idea what it is like to be her. If we both had implants with broadband links, she'd still be a mystery.

When I go back into the bedroom, she's still absorbed in the medieval-magic book. The red light glows on the digital recorder. Pick it up, put it on the bedside table, scooch over to her. "Baby, I have something to ask you."

She turns, peers at me over her cat-eye glasses. "What is it?" She puts the book down, takes her glasses off. She can tell something is up from my voice, no need for Intuition.

"Claire and Neal will both be in college soon." Tell her about my latest conversation with Neal? No, not now, too much of a digression, and she'll want to analyze that to death, she worries too much about my kids. "So there really won't be much keeping me in Cold Spring. And I was thinking that... maybe we should live together. I should move in with you."

"No, Honey, living together isn't a good idea." Immediately, as if she expected my question, and had her answer ready. "Things are good the way they are now. We're together when we want to be, but we also have time to ourselves. I think that's the perfect arrangement for us." She contemplates me. "I decided after Dwayne and I got divorced that I would never live with a man again. I love my freedom too much. Did you read that article I sent you last week about couples living together versus apart? Living apart is much better for romance. Couples like each other more, the relationship lasts longer, the sex is better. I mean, there's no comparison. It's scientific, Honey! You should appreciate that!" She laughs. "Oh my God, Eamon! I thought for a second you were going to ask me to marry you!" She studies me. "I think you should move to Hoboken, so you can be closer to me, and your school. I'll help you find an apartment and furnish it with stuff from Ikea. Make it sexy and stylish, so I'll want to visit you. Not like your sad little hovel in Cold Spring."

"Okay," I say. Okay? That's it? Where are words when I need them? "You know that if I lived with you, I'd pay you rent, whatever you think is fair."

"I should hope so! But we shouldn't live together to save money. The only question is what's good for us emotionally. And emotionally we're better off having our own places." She leans forward to scan my face more closely, then reaches out and strokes my arm. "Are you okay? You know I love you, right? I just can't be with you all the time."

I nod, once, twice, hoping to dislodge words. This is the moment for words, but how can I speak if I don't know what I feel? "I'm going to get some seltzer. You want some?"

"No thanks." She picks up her magic book.

Go into the kitchen, pour a glass of seltzer. Am I hurt or relieved? Can't decide. Free Will, what a joke. Go back into the bedroom, lie beside her. She's reading her book again.

"What would have happened if I came to one of those psychic fairs where you were giving a reading? Would you have told me that my marriage was breaking up? Because you wanted to hook up with me yourself? Instead of foreseeing the future, you would have been making the future happen. By seducing me!" Add with an Austin Powers leer, "Yeah, Baby!"

She gazes primly at me over her glasses. "No. I would never have done that. That would have been horrible. Unprofessional. Unethical."

"Even if you thought I was hot?"

"First of all, I take the cards very seriously. Also, I don't seduce guys, that's not my style. That's male porn fantasy, being seduced by the Gypsy Fortune Teller with the big boobs and low-cut blouse. Now stop bothering me. I want to finish this chapter."

Imagine Emily in a low-cut blouse waving delicate pale fingers over a crystal ball, her red-painted lips slightly parted, blue-shadowed eyes glancing up from her crystal ball into my eyes. Erection Detection getting a signal!

Grab my notebook off the bedside table, flip through pages covered with black ink, my Unabomber Scribbling, she calls it. Notes on today: Waking up, morning commute, class on William James, lunch with Jim and Dave and François, ferry ride, Hunger Memorial, kids playing soccer, Ice Cream Man, subway station. There's a vast gap between my handwritten descriptions and what I really saw, heard, felt. These are just stories, not truth. And what do they add up to? What's the point? Kicker? Payoff? I need an epiphany, insight, to sum up the day. Maybe acknowledge I can't see things as they really are, because I'm looking too hard for significance, metaphors, meaning. Nothing in my life is an end in itself, everything is just a means to meaning. No, not meaning, words. I'm just a writing robot, a contraption for turning experience into words, words that don't matter, because they will soon be forgotten, even by me.

No, too much of a downer. Try this: Everything is pointless, there's no reason for anything to exist, but here we are, we're lonely loving creatures, alone together on a great mystical adventure, headed for Heat Death, can't escape our fate, but that's okay, we can still hold hands and enjoy the ride, we can dance and tongue-kiss, like the merry girl and boy skeletons in my apartment, we can enjoy each other's company.

A cliché, but it could work. Everything is infinitely improbable, especially Emily, my girlfriend here on the bed beside me, with her Intuition and magic book, wearing her pink t-shirt and turquoise cat-eye glasses. Science cannot capture her, not even the most intricate mathematical model or algorithm. Poems and songs and paintings can't either. Nothing can. She is irreducible ineffable miraculous. I need her more than she needs me, and that's okay, that's as it should be.

Slide fingertips along her haunch. She frowns at her book. Say something romantic, but what? I tell her about walking to her apartment this afternoon, and making eye contact with Ice Cream Man, how it reminded me of my Big Drug Trip, when I *knew* all things are one. Finishing the story I say, "But I don't want to be one with all things. I don't even want to be one with you, Baby. I want to be *apart* from you, *different* from you, so I can love you, and cherish you."

Without looking up she responds, "Don't you worry about that. I am *completely* different from the likes of you."

"I just got this great idea for my stream-of-thought book," I say, rolling closer. "I'll end it with a scene in which you're reading some stupid magic book, and I'm trying to distract you by kissing your belly."

"The only thing stupid here is you, Mr. Magoo."

"I'll make that part of the scene, you calling me Mr. Magoo." I nuzzle her, and she doesn't push me away.

"What are you doing?"

"Gathering material for my book."

"Is that recorder still on, Monkey Man?"

THE END

About the Author

John Horgan is a science journalist and Director of the Center for Science Writings at Stevens Institute of Technology. His previous books are *The End of Science, The Undiscovered Mind, Rational Mysticism, The End of War* and *Mind-Body Problems*. He writes an online column for *Scientific American* and produces "Mind-Body Problems" for the online talk show Bloggingheads.tv.

Further Reading

You can find information on the ideas in this book in Horgan's online writings for *Scientific American* and in his other books. The one that most closely resembles *Pay Attention* in style and substance is *Mind-Body Problems: Science, Subjectivity and Who We Really Are*, which you can buy from Amazon or read for free at mindbodyproblems.com.